PUNK LAND

CARLTON
MELLICK

Eraserhead Press
Portland, OR

ERASERHEAD PRESS
205 NE BRYANT
PORTLAND, OR 97211

WWW.ERASERHEADPRESS.COM

ISBN: 0-9762498-4-7

AUTHOR'S NOTE

I was inspired to write Punk Land after I came across the website of a blue-haired model named Darenzia and a secret agent themed photoshoot she did with photographer Kyle Cassidy. I always wanted to write a Bizarro-style James Bond story, and after seeing Darenzia as a secret agent with a giant blue mohawk I was inspired to write it.

This was around the time Satan Burger started taking off and I was getting a lot of letters from readers asking for a sequel. I don't really like the idea of writing sequels to novels, but I did think it might be nice to write three 50-page stories explaining what happened to Satan, Mortician + Nan, and Leaf + Christian, then release them under one cover. Of the three ideas I had, the only one that really appealed to me was the one about Mort and Nan. I thought it might be funny if they ended up in Punk Land, the punk version of Heaven, which was mentioned briefly in Satan Burger. So I decided to combine the punk secret agent idea with the Punk Land idea.

But this book is not a sequel. It should stand alone. The two books are connected in small ways, but they don't have to be read in a specific order.

Besides being a follow-up to Satan Burger, this book is also a follow-up to my novel "The Cranky Dildo," which has been lost for good. It was about the character Goblin and his time spent in Heaven. It was a terrible thing losing this book. I'm never going to attempt to write it again, so it will never get published. Instead, I decided to put Goblin into Punk Land. Much of the plot of "The Cranky Dildo" is mentioned in this book, as Goblin's backstory, so at least it's not a total waste. By the way, you might be familiar with the title, "The Cranky Dildo," because it was also the name of a small press magazine I used to edit in the late 90's that featured stories of an absurd yet pornographic nature. It was much more lame than it sounds.

So here you go, Punk Land, my 11th book. I had a blast writing it. Hope you dig it and shit. Punch!

- Carlton Mellick III, 9/15/05 9:06 pm

This book is dedicated to this guy:

"Let's tune our weapons!"

—— Jon Mikl Thor

Thor

ACT ONE
THE GATES OF PUNK LAND

Scene One
Everyone In Heaven Is Deformed

☺

It's true. All of them. Deformed!
What, you don't believe me?
Well, just take my word for it. I was
there, only a few years ago.
In Heaven.

☺

There must be something terribly wrong
with the Pearly Gates. Some kind of electrical problem that God's handyman never
got around to fixing since the dawn of
mankind.
Because any human soul who passes
through these gates after its earthly de-
mise is instantly attacked with beams of
blue light (which make sound effects not
unlike lasers fired from Cylon warships in
the 1970's Battlestar Galactica television
series) that distort and mutate human ghosts
into sausage-hideous monstrosities. Only
God Himself looks human, as well as His
son, the Jesus Christ.
The Heaven-born angels can take any
form they wish, human-like or creature-
styled, but they normally make themselves

severely deformed so the earthly souls don't feel so bad about themselves . . . Even though God posts pictures of Himself all over the place, a constant reminder of how perfect He is.

Here is the picture God posts of Himself all over the streets of Heaven:

Not really an ugly guy, though not really attractive either. But He insists that His image is the definition of perfect.

Jesus doesn't have pictures of himself posted in the streets and malls, so I'm not sure what he looks like. I've never met anyone who was able to describe him to me, but I hear the old paintings of him on Earth are not at all accurate.

Somebody once told me Jesus left Heaven a long time ago for one reason or another. There's a rumor that he got in a huge fight with his dad and was nail-punched down to hell like Satan, to baby-sit all the damned souls who are rotting there. But I don't know for sure.

In Heaven, questions are often left unanswered.

☺

Let me introduce myself:

I am Goblin.

Well, that's what they told me my name was after I became deformed by passing through the Pearly Gates into Heaven.

I was born a Cal Corncob, I remember, and I used to ride bicycles and go to the mall and stomp on bugs and collect dildos and drink pizza from a tube, but then I died. I can't do much of anything now that I've died.

The attendants at the Pearly Gates told me: *You are Goblin*, so I figured they knew what they were talking about.

Cal Corncob was just my Earth name, because it was given to me by my parents. Goblin is my soul's name, because it was given to me by God. You see, God doesn't like the whole naming process on Earth. He said it is getting out of hand with all the Marys and Johns and Tims and Tonys and Sarahs and Nicks and Stephanies and Adams and Katies and Matts and so on. The identity confusion is mind-bumbling and God doesn't stand for anyone who bumbles as such inside of his or her mind, at least not in Heaven. So God names everyone different. Like me, I am the first and only Goblin. As you can guess, God is already running out of names.

I can't wait until He is so short of names that He is forced to name someone *Dildo*.

☺

I am not in Heaven anymore. They kicked me out.

I'm now in a place called *Punk Land*. It's the place where punks go after they die.

You see, several years ago, back when the punks started forming an anti-establishment subculture on Earth in the seventies, there were also some deformed punks in Heaven who started to rebel against God's way by wearing spikes and coloring their hair into green Mohawks and disrespecting the upper class and not caring about anything that God thinks they should care about.

Of course, the little Arab-like man did not accept their newfound behavior one bit. He told them that He will not stand for nonconformity in Heaven and threatened to kick them out.

In response, the deformed punks ate some cheeseburgers and then told Him to go masturbate with a spork.

"If we're not good enough for you, we'll make our own heaven," the punks said.

And God slicked back his thinning hair and put on a pair of Pierre Cardin sunglasses.

He said, with his God-accent (which is kind of like a cross between Greek and Klingon) "Your simple minds could never comprehend the complexity of building a heaven."

But the punks just Sieg Heiled him and marched straight out of the Pearly Gates into the beyond.

☺

Luckily, the exiting of the gates did not make them even more deformed than they already were. Another dose of deformation would create messy-fleshed blob-beings worse than the Elephant Man.

☺

I'm not sure how they created their own heaven, but they said it was extremely easy. Easier than building a house. And the only reason why other people didn't leave and start their own heavens is because God makes sure to keep his residents ignorant and afraid. Otherwise, there would be all kinds of heavens all over the god dimension.

Of course, to keep their heaven running, the punks needed to find their own god. Somebody to be like a leader.

They weren't all teen hooligans. Many were intellectuals, poets, philosophers,

Elvis, teachers, artists, and civil rights activists. But nobody wanted to be the god. It seemed like too much of a responsibility.

So they wandered a blank world for a while in search of someone to call their deity.

☺

By good fortune, they didn't have to search for very long. In fact, their god came to them.

He was a recently deceased young man, daze-wandering the blankness. Some strange force attracted Him straight to the group of exiled punks instead of to God. As if by destiny.

The young non-deformed punk said His name was John Simon Ritchie, but the punks on Earth knew Him as Sid Vicious.

When the deformed punks asked Him to be their god, He could hardly refuse them.

And before the end of that day, Punk Land was born.

Scene Two
The Cranky Dildo

☺

I was kicked out of Heaven for throwing a dildo at God.

I couldn't help myself. It was something that had to be done, and my desire to do it fairy-twitched throughout my entire body until I couldn't resist any longer.

It's because I have an obsession with throwing dildos at people. Especially the mammoth-sized ones, that are made for BIG comedy at orgy parties. I didn't mean any harm. It is just my way of showing affection. I tried to explain my ailment to the angels, but they didn't believe that dildophelia was a legitimate psychological disorder, so I was thrown out into the blankness, never to return to Heaven again.

There's just something genius about a dildo. Something that most people don't really understand. It is funny and shocking and was once a masturbation breakthrough, but there is something even more to it than that. Something that reeks of mystery and wonder, something more astonishing than words could ever explain . . .

At one point, before my death, I would ponder to myself: "If there is a God, I bet He is very much like a dildo."

☺

I used to have hundreds of dildos back when I was alive, when I was Cal Corncob.

In my dildo-collecting, I found many interesting varieties, but one of my favorites was the fist. A giant penis with a fist for a head. I guess I just liked funny-shaped sex toys, even though there weren't all that many around. Instead of always being penis-shaped, they should have made them snake-shaped or banana-shaped or car-shaped or tinyman-shaped. If I was still alive I would market the funny-shaped dildo and make millions of dollars. It would've been a BIG hit at orgy parties.

My dildo display, spread across a ping-pong table that took up nearly half of my living room, was designed to resemble a large city with penis-shaped skyscrapers. Roads and toy cars zigzag through the dildos, with miniature trees and sidewalks and pedestrians walking to work.

Nobody appreciated my dildo display or quite understood it. Well, I didn't really have any friends; I was horribly misunderstood. But I always wanted a friend to show my dildos to.

Sometimes I'd invite a coworker to my place for some beers and movies—I worked at a video store and although I was a lonely man, I could always cheer myself up by losing myself in any kind of movie—but

Funny-shaped dildos I would have invented:

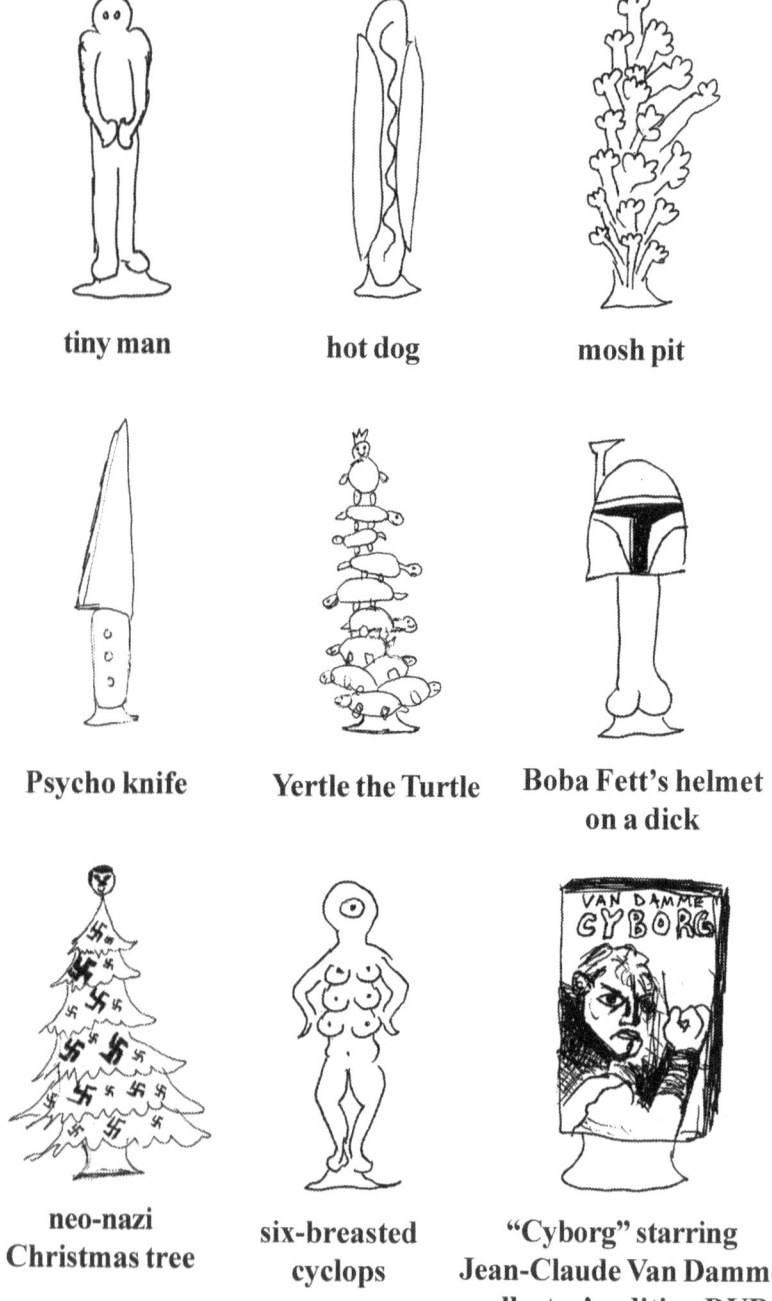

tiny man

hot dog

mosh pit

Psycho knife

Yertle the Turtle

Boba Fett's helmet
on a dick

neo-nazi
Christmas tree

six-breasted
cyclops

"Cyborg" starring
Jean-Claude Van Damme
collector's edition DVD

all the coworkers reacted badly to my sex toy display.

These coworkers (who were usually heavy metallers that all for some reason tried desperately to come off as tough ghetto thugs) would say something like, "What the hell's this, yo?"

And I'd respond, "Isn't it just brilliant!"

"Are those . . . dildos, yo?" they'd ask.

And I'd respond, "Yes, yes."

"Why do you have all these dildos, yo? Are you gay or something, yo?" They'd say.

"Gay? What do you mean?" I'd say.

"You put those in your butt, yo!" they'd cry. "You're a fucking homo, yo!"

"No, you don't understand," I'd say. "I do not use these for anal masturbation. They are my hobby. Like a stamp collection."

"But they're penis-shaped, yo. Only a girl or a gay guy would want to own them, yo!"

"No, no, no, they are much more than that," I'd say. "They are genius and divine!"

"Oh man, yo," they'd say. "You're such a faggy weirdo, yo!"

"I'm not weird. I'm just unique. I take pride in my dildo collection!"

But the conversation would never last any longer than that. The guy would walk out, fists clenched, a defensive retreat as if in danger of being attacked, and the next day he'd usually tell everyone at work to stay away from me. And everything would be uncomfortable and miserable in my life for a while, unless I was at home watching movies.

Luckily, when working at a video store, the entire employee staff besides myself changes every few months, so there was always another chance at making a friend.

☺

Oh yeah, and I guess throwing dildos at people from my apartment window didn't win me any popularity points with the neighbors . . .

☺

When I died, I didn't get to take my dildos with me.

I felt naked and humiliated without them, could hardly breathe (not that you need to breathe when you're dead, anyway) like my existence was caving in on me. I'd never felt more alone.

In Heaven, there are no dildos. Or at least that's what St. Peter told me, who always hangs out by the football stadium near the gates. His blobby features said, "There is no need for sex in paradise, and especially no need for sexual playthings."

"But I don't use them for sex," I told him.

His face was confuse-squished. He couldn't comprehend the greatness of dildos, either.

☺

"Heaven is larger than a thousand worlds," they say, but I only saw a very small part of it while I was there.

I was in the metropolis by the Pearly Gates, not sure if the city had a name, but it was designed to process the incoming souls like myself. It looked very much like a combination between Chicago and an extremely large outdoor mall, except the sky was always white and there weren't any streets or cars. Kind of a let down, actually. It seemed so simplistic. I was hoping for something much more grand in the afterlife. Something magnificent. But no, it was just a dildo-deficient shopping mall version of the bland world I left behind.

I was supposed to go through orientation after I died, but I never bothered attending. They set me up in a tiny one room apartment full of potatoes growing out of a pile of mulch on one side of the room. It was a cozy little place with one window and one door. But it always had a strong brown paper bag smell.

After they moved me in, I developed an instant case of agoraphobia due to the lack of dildos in my possession. There was nothing of interest to make me leave the apartment.

☺

All I did in Heaven, day after day (not that there ever was a night in Heaven since the sky was always paper-colored), was watch a monitor on the wall of my room, while sitting in a rickety chair and twiddling a blackened toothpick.

The monitor was like a television set, but instead of television shows they played the lives of the people living on Earth.

It was very amusing, almost more fun than the movies I used to watch when I was alive. You could see the world through their eyes or watch them through a floating pair of *God's Eyes*.

You could watch anyone you wanted. Presidents, movie stars, kung fu fighters, crocodile hunters, brain surgeons, professional wrestlers, secret agents, Nobel Peace Prize winners. But most of the time I just watched the lives of Thai prostitutes, and masturbated constantly.

Sometimes, between masturbations, I would watch my cousin Aggie. She was the only member of my family who didn't completely hate me, and then only person on Earth I gave a damn about.

She was a punk chick living in Rippington, New Canada, and was in love with a boy nicknamed *Boot Lips*. It was fun to watch her have fun, it made me happy to see her happy, her excitement became my excitement.

But it was kind of creepy to watch her private life. People sure fart a lot. And smell themselves. I didn't want to see that. And I sure as hell didn't want to see her fucking her boyfriend in the ass with a strap-on.

I tried to avoid witnessing her sex life, but she and Boot Lips were at it like rabbits half the time. And if Boot Lips wasn't around, she'd find somebody else to be his temporary replacement for a while.

I usually was able to change the channel before she took her shirt off, but I hated when I'd tune in to her life while she was in the middle of a fuck frenzy. It really made me feel dirty, even though I didn't turn to it on purpose.

Hopefully nobody watched me while I was alive. I wouldn't have been all that entertaining, so most people probably didn't watch more than a couple minutes. I guess my ancestors would've wanted to watch me as a kid, but they probably got sick of my channel once I reached puberty and started masturbating all the time. And my dildo obsession was probably far too much for them to stomach, even though I wasn't using them for sex.

I only got to watch Aggie's channel for a few weeks before the screen went fuzzy. There wasn't a picture on any channel for a few days and when it came back on it no longer played the lives of people on Earth. It just played reruns of *M.A.S.H.* and *Hee Haw*.

☺

Boredom clunked in enough that I got the bravery to leave my apartment for a few minutes at a time. I would go down to the lobby and ask random people questions, usually about what's wrong with the television, before running back upstairs to cry into the rotten potato mess I used for a bed. Nobody had any answers for me, but they all had twitchy white faces that made me very nervous. If they were thinking what I was thinking: something very horrible had happened on Earth.

The end of the world must have come. Not a human being left alive. Or perhaps God just didn't want us to see what was going on down there.

I didn't get the chance to find out for sure.

☺

Right now, in Punk Land, I'm holding a dildo in my arms like a baby.

I did manage to find a dildo in Heaven, after asking every angel I came across, most replying with grizzle-repulsed faces.

It turned out that God had at one point in time given a dildo a soul. It wasn't animated during its lifetime, just a normal latex dildo sleeping in a box during the day and swallowed up by a woman's vagina at night. But after it died, burned in a house fire, it's soul went up to Heaven to be with the angels. And in Heaven, the dildo was alive.

☺

It is calm in my arms, only wiggling a little bit. Its mouth wide open in a gentle snore. It looks and feels exactly like a dildo, but it can move and eat and talk. Well, it doesn't really talk. Its intelligence is that of a baby's, so it can only gurgle and burp and cry.

I named the dildo *Frog Strips,* after my first dildo that I gave away to my cousin as a Christmas present when I was sixteen. I always named my dildos, like pets or children, but never in my wildest dreams had I imagined having a live dildo as a pet/child.

Frog Strips is my everything. She is more like a pet than a baby, but I treat her like my daughter. She is my family, my love. The dildo is not female, dildos don't have reproductive organs, but I always find myself calling it a *she*. It seems very feminine, its gurgles are like female baby gurgles, and it is curvy like it has hips and the sides of breasts. Perhaps it really is a girl, the penis-hole like a little vagina.

☺

Frog Strips and I live all by ourselves in the guard house near the gates of Punk Land.

I'm the guardian of the gate and my job is to not let anyone in who isn't totally punk and shit.

These gates, however, do not make you deformed like the gates of Heaven do. They are just normal iron gates. Instead of being called the *Pearly Gates* they are called the *Oi, I'm Going To Punch You In The Head! Gates.*

Well, actually, they were never named that, they don't really have a name, but somebody spray-painted that message on a wall near the gate so that's how we refer

PEOPLE I KNEW WHEN I WAS ALIVE

Elaine - my mom. She was a child welfare social worker even though she hated helping people and she *really* hated children. But she did love being viewed as saintly, and if you failed to acknowledge this she would surely remind you. Her favorite activities included: smoking GPC menthols, selling garden gnomes on ebay, and bitching about how stupid people are.

Raoul - my mom's ex-boyfriend. She used to have to pick him up from gay bars every other night because he was too drunk to drive home. He would give her kittens as presents every time he fucked up, which was frequently. Her entire house was infested with hissy clawing cats until she dumped him and he demanded she give them all back. He also coached lacrosse at my school.

Steve - he was the manager of the video store I worked at. His favorite movies were Chuck Norris movies. Whenever somebody would rent an action movie he would try to convince them to get a Chuck Norris action movie instead. Whenever he said "Chuck Norris" he would wink at the costumer. He was always winking at people all the time.

Troy - he lived across the hall from me and used to blast Limp Biskit all the time. Once I dropped a dildo at him from my window when he was smoking in front of our apartment building. He thought one of the gangsta teens drinking 40s next to him did it and confronted them. After he got out of the hospital, he moved back in with his parents.

to them.

☺

I put Frog Strips to sleep in her pink-dotted caterpillar crib, tenderly, making sure not to touch the bruise on her hip. The bruise was formed when I threw her at God. It was a terrible thing for me to do to her, and I promised not to throw her at anyone ever again, but as I said, I just couldn't stop myself. It's been three years since I threw her at God, and she has yet to heal.

We heal very quickly in the afterlife. Even the most fatal wounding will mend itself in just hours or days; a severed limb will grow back like a lizard's tail. But Frog Strips' bruise never healed and probably never will. As if damage caused by God is eternal.

I kiss the dildo on the cheek and turn out the light. Walk out of the small brown-brick building and lock the door, hoping the baby doesn't wake from her nap while I'm gone.

It is a lonely walk from the guardhouse into town. The sky is always dark grey and the spiky metal trees shift in the stringy wind. My hobo clothes are not very warm, no matter how many layers I wear. I attempt to cover my flesh Mohawk with a red checkered scarf while slipping on wet rocks.

No one comes here anymore. No need to. There hasn't been a single soul to come through the gates of Punk Land in over a year. All the other gate attendants resigned their positions many months ago and the Punk Council didn't get anyone to replace them. So it's just me now. Me and Frog Strips. At the edge of the punk world.

Up ahead, is Coggly, the closest town to the gates. Most of the older and more deformed punks live there. It was the first town built after Sid Vicious created this realm from his imagination, and all the buildings there are old-crumbling with a smell similar to burnt cheese. But it is a quiet place and the only town in all of Punk Land that doesn't have loud punk shows every second of every day. It's the only place I ever really visit anymore.

☺

The air gets icy and particles of white collect along the sides of the stone road. Blister-nosed, I stagger into a quiet snowstorm.

Punk Land is always in a season similar to the middle of winter, but it rarely snows. Always cool, sometimes uncomfortably cold, but never like this.

As I enter Coggly, I find myself sledging through piles of flurry, trying to keep my balance with these horribly deformed legs. Most of my weight is on the right half of my body; horns of bone and meat mushroom out of my side, from my ribs to my knee, and a few on my shoulder. Damned by God's malicious gate.

The roads and rooftops are thick with white. Cemetery emotions. I pass darkened shacks, wandering through a maze-clutter of ruins.

The only light I can find is coming from a small window in Mully's Basement Tavern, dim and candle-lit.

☺

We can't get drunk off of alcohol in Punk Land because our bodies spit out toxins before we have a chance to enjoy them. But we do have a thing called *assihol*, which is some kind of strange battery acid-tasting fluid that jumbles up your senses and kind of reminds you of being drunk. It is much stronger than alcohol so our bodies can't process it as fast. And I've heard the hangovers can be nasty. Sometimes causing the heart to choke-up every other beat.

I drink small amounts on occasion, but I'm too scared of the hangover to drink enough to catch a decent buzz. I've been told it isn't really that similar to drinking alcohol. It is more similar to huffing gasoline.

☺

Bonk-staggering down the steps to the bar and trying to pull open the door. But it won't budge.

Rubbing the prickly slush from my eyes: a corpse lies at my feet, blocking the entrance.

☺

The corpse is a very deformed young man, eyes closed, in the snow.

"Come on, get up," I tell him.

But he doesn't move.

I pull on the door with all my weight until he slides away and there's enough room for me to squeeze inside.

He is not really dead. He is just pretending. We can't really die anymore. But a long time ago the Punk Council decided that civilization just isn't fun without death. Fear of death keeps us together and happy. So they made it a law that if your heart stops, for whatever reason, you are officially dead and have to lie down on the ground and pretend you are a corpse for awhile.

I have never had to pretend to be dead in Punk Land, luckily. I don't know how long you're supposed to just lie there, but it must be for a long time because I've seen corpses in the road just rotting there for days, trying not to move.

I'm surprised people actually do this. It's like playing guns on the playground as a kid, where nobody wants to feign death when shot with an invisible bullet. Following the rules means you miss out on all the fun.

And you'd think punks wouldn't follow anyone's rules.

☺

I wonder if dying hurts here as much as it does on Earth.

My original death was caused when my body was pushed into the path of an oncoming bus. I remember feeling my skull pop

Six things you should carry around with you at all times just in case you die:

1) Entertainment. A book, pad of paper, pocket tetris, or any type of solitary entertainment will help you pass the time while waiting to get picked up. Just make sure nobody is watching.

2) Snacks. A bag of peanuts or trail mix should do fine for satisfying hunger, but make sure you also have a bottle of water or can of soda to wash it down with.

3) Catheter Bag. You might not have had to go to the bathroom before you died, but after lying there for a while you'll inevitably have to go sooner or later. It's best to have a catheter bag or empty bottle handy for such an occasion.

4) Sleeping Pills, Type A (concentrated assihol). If you're waiting around for a day or longer you're going to have to get some sleep. Not everyone is lucky enough to die in a comfy bed. You'll most likely require a sleep aid. Carry as many of these as possible. They are also helpful in relieving pain.

5) Warm Clothes. Just in case you die in chilly weather, it's best to have some warm clothing. Wearing a hat also helps if you die under sunshine or bright lights.

6) Alarm. The most useful item to carry around with you is some kind of noise-maker that will create awareness of your situation. A beeper, alarm clock, boombox . . . anything that creates noise continuously will work.

DEATH CAN STRIKE AT ANY TIME. BE PREPARED.

open and my face forced through the grill like a cheese grater. I died quickly, but the pain resonated through my ghost after I passed on to the other side.

I knew exactly what happened to me. I knew I was dead. Most people entering Punk Land or Heaven are confused and have no idea what has happened to them, but everything was clear to me. VERY clear. My senses were more clear than they had ever been in life. Especially my sense of pain, because all of my soul was writhing in needle-ripping agony, like the nerves in my flesh had caught fire. Like I had been skinned alive.

☺

Inside of Mully's, there is plenty of warmth but not much liveliness.

The candle-lit room contains only one soul. A guy named Mox, who lives next door to the bar.

Purple moss grows in the windows and on the table-tops. A bowl of chitter shrimp are fizzing in a tub next to the bar.

"There's a corpse out here," I tell him.

Mox grunts out of a daze and uprights his assihol glass.

"Want to help me bring him in?" I ask. "It's freezing out there."

A black beetle crawls out of his hand.

"Let him freeze," the man says. "If it's too cold for him he'll eventually come inside and re-die."

☺

"Where's Mully?" I ask the drinking and grumbling-to-himself man.

Mox is an older punk who died only recently but was part of the original punk scene. He's white-haired and balding, a nose like a rose bush, but still heavily pierced and tattooed.

His clothes: sweat/dirt-stained denim.

Like any other old man (actually, he was not even middle-aged when he died but drugs and misuse took a huge toll on his body, so much that he appears close to elderly) he's very bitter about everything and only wants to sit around and drink and bitch.

"Gone," Mox blorps. "All gone. Some dead people are lingering, but the others went somewhere else."

"Somewhere else?" I ask the old punk.

But the old guy wrinkles his face at me until I go back home.

Scene Three
The Complete Idiot's
Guide to Being Punk

☺

The bell is ringing outside and skins me from my tongue-wrapped sleep.

My face is too heavy to rise more than an inch from the rabbit pillow. Too warm, comfortable, bundled flappy-fleshed in my blanketpile I use for a bed. So I won't go to see who it is.

Probably just another door-to-door punk band, begging people to listen to their demo tape.

☺

I try to fade back into the world of dreams, hoping the bell-ringing will become like white noise.

I inhale the burnt pecan smell that sweats from the ceiling.

This room is very small, a windowless office/closet with brown-brick walls and patchwork fur carpeting. Just my bed/sheet-pile, a box of books, an oil lamp, and the crib containing Frog Strips.

Hard black crust in my nose like a rotting tumor crawling down from my brain.

My dreams always contain these things:

1) a woman named Tekky.
2) blue flesh art.
3) the sausage zoo.

The first, Tekky, is someone I knew when I was alive on Earth. I try never to think about her but she manages to sneak her way into my dreams every night. Sometimes playing the part of a character in a dream's storyline or maybe just a background character, but she's always there, haunting me.

The blue flesh art also haunts me. I guess the only way to explain blue flesh art is that it's living art made from blue human flesh, and it's the only kind of art that I can ever find in my dreams. Blue flesh paintings hanging on walls or blue flesh sculptures in the park. Once I made love with a blue flesh sculpture until my belly unzipped and internal organs slipped out onto the pavement. It was kind of a fun dream.

As for the sausage zoo, it is actually a real place here in Punk Land. It is like a regular zoo, but instead of animals the zoo is full of animal-shaped sculptures made out of processed meats. There aren't many animals in Punk Land, so a group of people decided to make a totally punk rock zoo that would be even better than any real zoo because the animals were going to be

A BLUE FLESH SCULPTURE

made out of sausage and bologna and hamburger and crap like that. It is a celebrated attraction around here. If you ever play a show at the sausage zoo, your band will definitely be considered the ultimate Mr. T (AKA coolest/toughest).

In other words: SAUSAGE = PUNK.

In my dreams, the animal sculptures are made out of the meat of the animal each sculpture is portraying. For example, the zebra sculpture is made out of zebra sausage. The hippo is hippo sausage. The peacocks are ground peacock.

It is like the punks, after death, have felt remorse for butchering animals for food during their lifetimes, and decided to now put them back together again. Into uncooked animal-shaped meatloaf things. Returning their meat back to their original forms.

☺

I awake dizzy-brained to the dildo blob-crying in her crib.

I light the lamp and go to Frog Strips, but freeze mid-air.

In the corner of my eyes I see two dark forms twitching in the doorway. They are strangers, intruders, covered in snow and wet blankets.

My muscles go stiff, my eyes lock on them. They don't speak, just shiver at me, not even showing their faces.

"Who are you?" I ask, lowering my

hands into the crib to warm Frog Strips.

They shiver at me.

Frog Strips purrs back into sleep.

"If you're wanting me to listen to your crappy demo tape you've come to the wrong place," I say. "We don't even have electricity to play it out here."

They don't respond.

I walk past them into the pepper-scented lobby, a large room for processing souls.

They left the doors open, ice blowing all over the tiles and iron benches. The two hobos zombie-follow me like I have food for them when I close and lock the door.

☺

Breaking the silence:

"You didn't answer the door," one of them crackle-says, chittery words that I can just barely understand. "We thought the place was deserted, like the old town at the end of the road."

They are wretched.

Even though their faces are hidden under blankets and shadows, I can still see that recent hardships have weakened them into these pathetic creatures.

What am I going to do with them?

☺

"Christ," I say. "You're not allowed in here, but . . ."

Their eyes swollen at me.

"All the guard rooms are empty," I

say. "You can stay until the storm passes as long as you don't leave a mess. Everything in this building is the property of The Council."

They shiver at me.

"There's some extra clothes and blankets in the back," I say. "Follow me."

☺

I take the two vagrants through the hallway and office maze to the living quarters, very tiny rooms where the guards used to live, where I used to live before I moved into the slightly larger storage room by the lobby.

Actually, I didn't move out of my quarters because I wanted more space. I have been avoiding this entire wing of the building for a very long time.

A friend of mine, the only friend I have in Punk Land, was gutted here by an angry incoming skinhead soul who didn't take very well to being dead.

My friend—Grak was his name, a name given to him by God—came with me here to Punk Land from Heaven. We got jobs as gate attendants together, explored Punk Land together, were taught in the ways of this world together. We weren't extremely close. He had other friends, some that he spent most of his free time with. But, to me, he was my best friend.

And now he's gone.

He didn't really die, being immortal and all, but he's gone anyway. Some punk doctors took his pretending-to-be-dead corpse to a hospital somewhere so he could regenerate in safety for a while. It happened too quickly for me to really know what was going on. I just got to see his guts on the floor, which I believe were never cleaned up, rotting and stinking up his office.

This was quite a long time ago and I have no idea what has become of him. I'm guessing it takes a very long time to regrow all of your internal organs. Or maybe he is all better but got another job in one of the large cities.

Or perhaps some people really do die here, permanently, but it's something no one ever likes to talk about.

☺

In the guard's lounge:

The two drifters do not change into the clothes I gave them, the Propagandhi shirts and jeans. They just strip to their underwear and wrap themselves in blankets. I hang their soggy clothes by the fire to dry.

They are maybe a few years younger than me, late teens or early twenties. But I've never been very good with guessing ages. One is an Asian guy and the other is a boyish girl.

I give them soup and crackers and they gobble the food down before I can pour them cups of milk and give them each a Nutter Butter for dessert.

"In the town back there we saw people lying in the road," says the guy, who speaks in an accent like a cross between Japanese and Pirate. "They weren't dead. They were just lying there, in the snow. Not even asleep. It was like they were pretending to be dead or something."

My eyes twist confused at the man's words. They should know there are people pretending to be dead all the time.

It's almost as if they are . . .

"Are you newcomers?" I ask him.

He doesn't understand.

"You don't seem like you're from here," I say. "Did you just arrive?"

They look at each other, then look back at me, and half-nod.

But how could they be new? There aren't new souls coming in here anymore. I didn't hear them open the gates—a noise that is impossible for me to miss or sleep through. It's like a rumbling deep in my lungs when the gate opens.

"Did you come through the gates?" I ask.

They shake their heads.

"How long have you been here, in Punk Land?"

"Punk Land?" they ask, giggling. "*The* Punk Land?"

"You *are* newcomers, aren't you? But you didn't come through the gates? Perhaps you've been here for years but have amnesia . . ."

Does amnesia even exist here?

They pause at me. Then the girl says, "We arrived maybe twenty hours ago. Came from over the mountains."

"But, I don't understand, how?" I say, my dangling fleshparts flap at them. "There's no way to get into Punk Land except the gates."

"We came through a doorway called The Walm," the Asian man says. "Our world was dying so we needed a place to go. It brought us here."

"You're saying you're from a different dimension?" I ask.

"I don't know," the guy says. "We are from a place called Earth. It might be another planet or another dimension. We don't know."

"Earth?" I say. "We are all from Earth. I believe you are confused. Most newcomers come here confused. Let me get some hot cocoa and I'll explain everything to you."

☺

They are mostly dried off and warmed by the fire. No longer shivering. Their hair crispy on their heads.

"This is going to be hard for you to grasp," I tell them. "But the both of you are dead."

They drink cocoa.

"This place we are in is called Punk Land," I say. "It is the place where punks go after they die. Everyone here has lived on Earth at one point in time, but have died and now their souls live here eternally."

The girl yawns.

The Asian man says, "Why are you deformed?"

I'm thrown off by the question and pinch at the air for a while. Then, I continue, "I'm not sure why you didn't come through the gates. Perhaps The Council has created a more high-tech gate that I am not familiar with. Were there any buildings by this gate? Any people? Was there somebody named Grak?"

"No," the girl says. "We were in the middle of nowhere. You're the first person we've seen who wasn't pretending to be dead."

The Asian guy says, "We destroyed The Walm from this side. There were one or two of our friends who were supposed to follow us through, but they never made it. They either went to a different place or stayed on Earth. We waited almost an entire day for them, before ripping the structure down. Luckily there weren't any of those Movac people to stop us."

"Walm? Movac?" My eyeballs are spinning at them.

"The Walm is an evil doorway created by God so people could travel between dimensions," the girl says.
"But it is fueled by the souls of humans. We had to destroy it or else this world would have ended up like Earth."

"What happened to Earth?" I ask.

"It's over," she says.

I spit into an empty soup bowl. There must be some kind of validity to their story. They don't seem all that delusional and their story does explain how they got here without coming through the gates. It also would explain why God wouldn't let us watch the Earthly television shows in Heaven, and why not a single punk has entered Punk Land for such a long time.

I begin to worry about my cousin, Aggie.

"So there is no one left alive on Earth?" I ask.

"In a way, we're the only survivors," the girl says.

☺

They say they've heard of Punk Land already, and that many punks on Earth believe in it. I'm not exactly sure how so many punks could know of the existence of Punk Land before death. Unless many of them had near-death experiences and saw the *Oi! I'm Going To Punch You In The Head! Gates* before going back to their Earthly bodies. There are rumors that G. G. Allin, a punk icon made famous by taking craps on stage and singing in the nude, was actually a punk messiah who spread the word of total anarchy to the punks on Earth. Perhaps, if G. G. Allin is like the punk version of Jesus, he had some kind of messiah magic that could not only help him sing naked and take dumps on stage but could also help him see into the Punk Land dimension like a clairvoyant.

☺

If they plan on staying, they'll have to be registered in the Punk Land directory. I take them into an office, light a sticky oil lamp, and open a dusty blank file from a stack of mildewy papers.

"Not just everyone will be allowed to stay here in Punk Land," I tell them, dipping a pen tip in my mouth. "You'll have to pass a series of tests to prove your punkitude."

"Punkitude?" the girl asks with curled eyebrows.

"What are your names?" I ask them, pen and paper in hand.

"Nan Bradley," the girl says.

"Mort Gonzalez," the guy says, "But they call me Mortician."

I write the names down in their files.

"Cool," I say to Mortician. "You have a totally punk nickname so you get two points. You need to get over 100 points to be accepted into Punk Land."

"You think his nickname is punk?" Nan asks. "What's so punk about having a nickname?"

"Those are the rules," I say.

"Rules?" Nan squirms.

"The rules of punk," I say.

"Punk doesn't have any rules," Nan says. "The whole point of punk is to break rules."

"You know not what you speak," I say.

"Christ, what a log of boob shit," Nan says.

☺

I hand them each a copy of The Complete Idiot's Guide to Being Punk.

This is what it looks like:

If you aren't totally punk rock then you better get a life and read this book right now.

-Ariel LeVera
        Punk Council Rep

Being Punk

by Johnny Rotten

* **An inviting introduction** to all the latest punk, anarchist, and skinhead trends

* **Popular strategies** for mastering mohawks, moshing, and rebellion.

* **Clear photos** to guide you through the most important aspects of punk fashion and attitude.

"This is your bible," I say to them. "All the rules and laws of Punk Land are in this book."

Nan looks down at the yellow cover. "Are you joking?"

I say, "You'll have to memorize all of that tonight, though a true punk would already know it by heart. In a few hours you'll be tested on it."

They groan at me.

"I refuse to take the test," Mort says in his weird piratey voice. "That should be proof enough that I am punk."

"Well, disobeying me will give you ten points," I say. "But you could get up to 120 points by answering all these test questions correctly."

Mort lowers his head.

"Okay," I scratch my head. "How many body modifications do you each have?"

"None," Mort says. "Body modification is stupid and trendy."

"That's too bad," I say. "You can get up to fifty points for each one."

"How about you?" I ask Nan.

"Ten on my back," Nan says. "One on my skull, one on my ass, three on my stomach, two on my tits . . . Seventeen total."

"Very, very good," I say. "Are any of them punk?"

"You tell me. *You're* the expert."

"I mean do you have any anarchy tattoos?" I say. "Those are worth fifty."

"My hair is a little grown out," she says, "but normally when my head is shaved you'd be able to see the words *blonde hair* tattooed on my head instead of hair."

"You get five points for that," I say.

"Only five points!" she says. "You'd give fifty for an anarchy symbol but only five for my blonde hair tattoo?"

I try to calm her down.

"You're such a mongoloid!" she says.

Many people who come through here are like her. They think they are punk but don't at all meet the Punk Guide's standards.

"All minor body modifications are worth five points," I say. "So, no worries, you're up to 85 points. But your blonde hair tattoo is not on the list of extra special punk rock tattoos. A Sid Vicious tattoo would also be worth 50 points. So would a Misfits skull. And any punk band names or song lyrics can also add up to quite a bit."

"One is a tattoo of the Knight Rider car on my ass," Nan says, BIG smile.

I shake my head at her and she frowns.

"Unfortunately, I can't give you any points for your clothes," I say. "You weren't wearing any spikes or punk band t-shirts and your hair wasn't multi-colored. You weren't even wearing a single bullet belt."

"Bullet belt!" Mort cries. "I wouldn't wear a bullet belt even if I became the lead singer of a black metal band!"

"Bullet belts are worth thirty punk points," I say. "Your clothes weren't punk at all. Why were you wearing such conservative clothing anyway?"

"Those were our work uniforms," Mort

says. "From Satan Burger."

"Oh cool," I tell them. "That's a fast food chain, right? I'll give five more points to each of you. Working for corporations is punk."

Nan wrinkles her face at me.

"Now I *know* you're full of shit," Nan says. "Did you really just fucking say working for corporations is punk? This is beyond stupid. How the hell did you get into Punk Land anyway? You're as punk as a Mormon."

I don't make eye contact with her.

Mortician mumbles something under his breath that sounds like, "Mormons are totally punk."

☺

I probably wouldn't have made it into Punk Land if I'd have come some time within the past couple years.

When I came, it was before the Punk Council, and everything was different. There wasn't a guide to being punk and the guards at the gate were really easygoing with who they let in. They believed the definition of 'punk' was very subjective, and that the punkest people of all were the ones who did not believe themselves to be punk. Like Mr. T.

I came from Heaven with Grak, as I said. Grak was not thrown out of Heaven like I was, but was sick to death of the place and wanted a change. He wasn't necessarily punk in life, but after his death he started to watch television shows of

punks on Earth and developed a similar
mindset. So, when I was publicly humiliated after my trial, and the angels were
escorting me and Frog Strips out of Heaven,
Grak followed me out of the gates and helped
direct me to the place that existed somewhere between Heaven and Hell.

☺

I was interviewed by a dreadlocked
Italian punk with a Bolt Thrower t-shirt.
The interview lasted only few minutes. He
told me that it was punk to be deformed,
and that I happened to be deformed in the
coolest way he's ever seen. My head has a
flesh mohawk that I always thought made me
look like a rooster. But the interviewer
said it was the toughest mohawk he's ever
seen, even more so than the guys with the
metal mohawks. And my right side has horns
of bone and flesh that he compared to metal
spikes. He said I had a very original look.
Very punk.

But the thing that really got me into
Punk Land was Frog Strips. I showed him my
little girl and asked if my dildo could
come in with me.

His eyes just lit up at Frog Strips,
at the idea of a dildo with a soul. He said
I was the most fascinating person he'd
seen in months, and the most punk by far.
If they had punk points back then, he would
have given me two hundred at least. I
couldn't believe it myself, but this guy
and a lot of the other punks in Punk Land
seemed to share a similar opinion of dildos

with me.

In other words: DILDOS = PUNK.

☺

By the end of the night, Nan has 126 punk points, and Mortician has 65.

"So you're going to kick me out?" Mort asks.

I am supposed to kick him out.

But I hesitate, thinking back to the dreadlocked punk who was kind enough to let me through the gates even though I am not at all a punk.

"No," I say. "No . . . you are on probation. You're just not a citizen yet. You have to study the punk guide and retake the test."

"Study this stupid book?" Mort says, holding up the yellow book as if preparing to hit me in the face with it.

"It's the only way," I say.

Nan pats him on the ear. "Just read the book and pass the stupid test. There's no place else to go."

☺

Some time passes, the two newcomers still wear blankets and refuse to put on any of the punk T-shirts I have taken out of the supply closet for them. Even the anarchy shirts aren't good enough for them, because they said the shirts are the same kind that they sell at the mall. Mort is busy groaning after every passage he reads in The Complete Idiot's Guide to Being

Punk, while Nan is following me around asking questions about the world she has just entered.

She asks, "How does this place exist? Why?" and I tell her about the rebellious Heaven punks and Sid Vicious, the god of Punk Land.

She asks, "What is this Punk Council?" and I tell her it is our government, the people who give law and order. It is made up of the punkest punks around. The ones who set the punk standard for everyone else.

She asks, "Did The Council write the punk guide?" and I tell her that a man they call Johnny Rotten wrote the book, he is the main spokesperson for The Council, and the most punk.

She asks, "Isn't Sid Vicious on the Punk Council?" and I tell her that Sid Vicious is like the President of Punk Land and The Council is like Congress. But Sid Vicious hasn't been in the public eye since the Punk Council was created. They do a lot of the work for Him. He is mostly just an icon these days.

☺

Then she asks me if she is allowed to keep her boyfriend's hand.

"What do you mean?" I respond.

She pulls a human hand out of her underwear. "My boyfriend is dead and I want to keep his hand."

I don't know how to respond to her, looking down at her little-boy face, looking innocently back at me as if severing off a dead loved one's body part is as normal as setting flowers by a grave.

But I jerk away when the hand begins to move.

I scream.

"His name is Breakfast," she says, petting the spidery hand/creature in her arms. "It is a demon hand. My boyfriend is gone, but I still have Breakfast. I treat him like my pet or my baby."

My eyes light up, "Like Frog Strips!"

"Frog Strips?" she kisses the hand on its palm/belly.

"I have an animated dildo that is like my child or my pet," I say.

"An animated dildo!" she says.

"Come see," I say. "It is already morning and about time for her to eat. We've been awake all night!"

"I won't be able to sleep for days," Nan says.

"Days!" I say, bobbing my head in amazement at the animated hand.

☺

I tell Nan the story of how Frog Strips came to be, how she is the first dildo with a soul and how I was kicked out of Heaven for throwing her at God.

"At God, you say!" Nan says, wasp-giggling.

"God!" I reply.

Our voices are high-strung for some reason. We must be delirious. Either from lack of sleep or because we are in shock.

Not sure.

I wake Frog Strips and cradle the dildo in my arms. It coos at me and sucks on my nose.

Nan shakes her head. "That is the sickest thing I have ever seen!"

By the smile on her face, I presume that was a compliment.

☺

We carry our little ones to the kitchen and make oatmeal for the living dildo and the living hand. They eat together on the counter top and make bubble-sounds at each other like it's friendly conversation.

Nan lies her head on her shoulder and sighs at the kids. A small tear in her eye.

"I like him," I say about Breakfast. "He's like Thing on Adam's Family."

"No," Nan says. "More like Bruce Campbell's demon hand in Evil Dead 2."

☺

We don't really need to sleep but our souls crave rest consistently. After a long morning of coffee and collecting rusty nails and watching our animated pets/babies play together, with Mort studying and flipping off his book in preparation for the test, we are all ready to collapse. Eyelids sliding down on their own, brain going into fuzzy jumble-thoughts . . .

Nan puts Breakfast and Frog Strips into the baby crib together. She kisses them goodnight and smiles at me.

There is something terribly wrong with

this girl.

☺

"She's changed all of a sudden," Mort tells me, after Nan hugs the two of us and goes into a cold closet/bedroom to sleep.

"Has she gone insane?" I ask him.

"It's been crazy for us lately. Her boyfriend just died. Not just his body, but his soul died as well. On Earth, a lot of people's souls were destroyed, eaten by The Walm just so they wouldn't go to Heaven after they died because there isn't any room there anymore. God figured the souls would be better used as fuel."

"But the souls could have come to Punk Land," I say. "Or to other places in the god dimension, if there are any."

"I was told that God wanted them as fuel. He probably thinks He owns the souls since He created the Earth, and doesn't want them coming to Punk Land or any other place that He doesn't control."

Mortician grabs his clothes from the fireplace in the lounge and dresses. Then makes a bed on a woolly couch.

☺

"So what was Heaven like anyway?" Mort asks.

"Like a giant shopping mall," I say.

Scene Four
Fairy-Drinking Cunts

☺

I do not dream of blue flesh or sausage animals for the first time in months, but I do dream of Tekky again. She is not playing a role in a dream-story; she's the same old Tekky, crazy-eyed with the end of her shirt pulled up into her teeth, playing with masked action figures on her bare belly and sticking their feet into her navel like it's some kind of man-eating hole in the ground.

"Let's go see a movie," I tell her from the kitchen table.

"No," she puffs her green lips at me, "I'm playing now."

☺

Tekky was a suicide girl. At least that's what she called herself. She had black and green hair with matching make-up, pink and white clothes, olive-colored skin. All she really did was hang out on my couch, watch cartoons, and eat cereal.

She was living on the streets, sleeping in video arcades when I met her, and was really good at flirting money out of teenagers and college guys.

I would encounter her every day on the way home from work, sitting on the steps by the skate park and drinking Yoohoo or chewing on a candy necklace. Always begging, and very persistent with her begging.

I would normally get flirted with or teased all the way down the street until I gave her something. She didn't care what. If I said I had no money she would ask for food. If I said I had no food she would ask for a cigarette. If I said I had no cigarettes she would ask for a pencil or some paper. If I said I had no pencil and paper she would ask for a lock of my hair or a scab. She would get something out of me each and every day, even if it was just some garbage in my pockets.

One day she didn't want any money or any food, she wanted a place to stay. I tried to ignore her, but she followed me all the way to my apartment and when we got to my front door I didn't know what to do.

She just rubbed against me like a stray cat and when I unlocked the door she walked inside ahead of me. Without me ever saying a word.

"What is this?" she asked, looking at my cityscape display of dildos.

She was the only woman to ever enter my apartment and see my dildo collection. I told her all about my obsession with dildos and she didn't even accuse me of being gay.

"I think I'm falling in love with you," she said, rubbing a lime green dildo against her cheek.

☺

She was in my bedroom and nodding in approval at my large round bed and shelves of MASK action figures and vehicles that I had acquired in college to get even with my parents for never buying them for me when I was a kid.

MASK was a popular but short-lived cartoon and toy line that tried to combine two other much-more-popular toy lines: G.I. Joe and Transformers, both of which are considered punk (though Joes are more commonly associated with punk girls, who sometimes collect the Zarana and Baroness figures). The MASK figures were like midget G.I. Joes, with removable helmets. The entire toy series based its design on the theory that kids like action figures with removable helmets. And also like automobiles that change into hi-tech things like robots. So, of course, the MASK vehicles could change from regular cars and motorcycles into hi-tech flying/hovering/rocket-shipping death machines. And I just loved them . . . even though I never got one for Christmas as a kid and didn't really have any friends who would let me play with theirs.

So I bought a bunch of them when I was all grown up. I kept them on shelves in my apartment bedroom, and sometimes played with them even though I'd feel guilty and stupid while doing so.

M.A.S.K. was some Mr. T shit

☺

Anyway, back to Tekky, she was in my bedroom and liked all of my toys and race car bed sheets and said, "Wow this is great! Not a bad place to spend the night at all."

Then gave me a *but where are you going to sleep?* face.

I still hadn't uttered a single word to her yet, and did not for the entire night. She made a bed for me on the couch and kissed my cheek goodnight and shut her bedroom door.

It was still early in the evening so I had the entire night to pretend I was alone. I couldn't sleep. I couldn't concentrate on the movies I had taken home from my video store. I was all nerves.

She seemed safe enough. I wasn't worried she was going to kill me in my sleep. I had no valuables for her to steal, except maybe my television. But I doubted she could even lift that thing—I had to pay two street workers downstairs $30 each to move it up here for me—so there was nothing at all I had to worry about. She just needed a place to stay and would leave the next morning.

In the morning, she didn't leave. I managed to fall asleep for a couple hours after the sun came up and was awakened by her butt plopping down on top of my knees to watch television.

"Thundercats are on!" she said, clicking the remote through the channels to find the Thundercats, even though they haven't played that cartoon since MASK was popular.

I watched cartoons with her until I had to go to the video store, which was the first time I had actually said a word to her.

I said: "I have to go to work."

But she didn't want to leave.

"I'll guard the apartment while you're gone," she said.

I didn't know what to do, so I left her in my apartment.

On the way out, she said, "Make sure to pick up some cereal on the way home. Fruity Pebbles and Circus Fun."

Even though they haven't made Circus Fun in years.

☺

After work, I picked up some cereal just in case she was still at my place. There wasn't any Fruity Pebbles to be found, but I did get her Chocolate Rice Crispies, Marshmallow Maties, and Crunch Berries. Though I was half-expecting to find my apartment completely bare and/or destroyed upon arrival.

Strangely enough, she was in the exact same spot I left her in: watching cartoons on the couch. But she was now wearing my boxer shorts and a Krabathor shirt.

I was a BIG fan of brutal death metal when I was younger and Krabathor was one of the brutalest, but I don't remember ever buying a Krabathor shirt. I can't begin to imagine what things of mine she had been digging through to find it.

The pink and white clothes that she was wearing were scattered all over the living room floor as well as a wet towel plopped over the dildo display table, a few of the sky scraper dildos lying on their sides.

"You brought it!" she said to me, kissing me on the cheek and taking the cereal boxes away. For some reason, I was worried she would be angry I didn't get Fruity Pebbles.

"I like you!" she said, digging through the Crunch Berries in search for a prize. "I'm going to stay here forever!"

☺

So, from that day on, Tekky lived with me and became my girlfriend. Well, I guess I liked to think of her as my girlfriend. She treated me more like a cute puppy dog than a boyfriend or a lover. We slept in the same bed together, but never made love. She would kiss me all over my body like she would a kitty, but never on my lips, never a serious kiss.

And when she was horny, she would take a razor blade or steak knife and cut her arms, the tops of her thighs, naked on my kitchen floor. Masturbating.

It grossed me out, so I didn't like to watch, but sometimes she made me watch. She'd lock us in the bathroom and sit against the door so I couldn't get out. Sometimes she would cut me while masturbating, and lick the wounds until I stopped bleeding. This is the closest I had ever come to sex.

The most intimacy I've ever had with another human being.

And I hated it.

☺

A few months after she moved in, Tekky said that we were far enough into our relationship for her to tell me about her deep secrets. Even though we were still complete strangers to each other and hardly ever communicated at all. She was in her own little world most of the time and only acknowledged me on rare occasions. It was like we were little kids pretending to play house.

She told me about her passions. She said she was a comic book artist and refused to work a job of any kind unless it had something to do with illustrating comic books. But she never had her art published, or studied art, or even showed her art to anyone. Though she wanted to show me, like I was special to her or something.

The comic book she was working on was called *Fairy-drinking Cunts*.

"It's a graphic novel," she told me.

I looked through her pages and pages of comic art, drawn on all kinds of paper: from backs of photocopies she got out of the recycle bin at the library, to notebook paper she flirted out of high school kids, or the backs of fliers from the record stores or taken off of street posts. Some of the drawings were even done on napkins or used paper plates. And they were drawn in several mediums from pencil to black, blue, red, green, even purple pen ink, magic marker, chalk, charcoal, crayon, and even blood.

"What do you think?" she asked.

All the pictures were crudely drawn and pornographic. They were mostly close-ups of vaginas eating pixies and fairy people. There wasn't dialogue or storyline to the images, even though she called it a graphic novel. Just drawing after drawing of fairy-swallowing cunts.

I looked in her eyes and saw that she was shaking. She was excited and nervous to hear what I had to say about her life's work.

My eyes went down to the drawings and searched potently for some kind of redeeming value in the images. They showed some talent, better than I could do, but not at all good enough to be published by anyone anywhere.

I looked back into her brown and yellow eyes and got goo-shivers.

For some reason I responded, "They are the best drawings I have ever seen in my life."

And her face exploded with smiles and tears, and she wrapped her arms around me and kissed me all over.

"I love you, I love you, I love you!" she said to me.

Even though I sounded far from sincere.

☺

I try not to think about Tekky any-

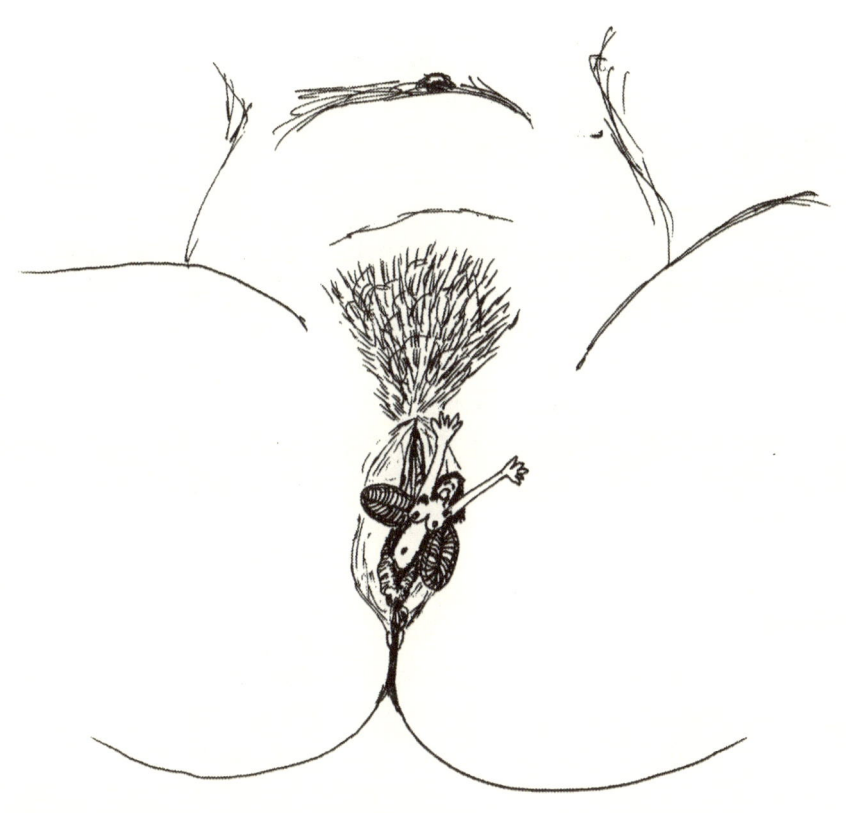

Tekky's masterpiece

more, but I can never find a way to stop
myself. She plagued my thoughts back when
I was alive and she still plagues my thoughts
now.

If only I could figure out a way to
stop dreaming, I would be free. If only I
could make my subconscious forget.

☺

It's the next day:

Mortician takes the punkitude test
again and fails.

"This is bullshit," he whines.

Nan, still using a blanket instead of
clothes, drinks her morning coffee with
Breakfast and Frog Strips in her lap, "Let
me give you tattoos. I just need a sewing
needle and some ink."

"I hate tattoos!" Mort says.

"I can just give you a stupid anarchy
symbol on your ass," Nan says. "Then you
will have enough punk points to become a
citizen."

She flashes her papers and new license at him, a citizenship wristband not
unlike the ones you'd get at a nightclub to
prove you're over 21.

"I'm not letting you put needles in my
ass," Mort says.

"It won't work anyway," I tell them.
"You're dead. You can't get tattooed anymore. Not permanently, at least. Only the
tattoos you got in life will carry on through
eternity. New ones just wash off."

"We told you," Nan says, "we never
died. We came through a doorway."

"It might be hard for you to accept it at this time," I say, "but you are dead. If you don't believe me then try to give him a tattoo. It will wash off just like a cheap temporary sticker tattoo that you'd find in a cereal box."

Mort shakes his head.

"I'll get you a needle," I say to Nan.

☺

She is giving him the crappiest anarchy tattoo I've ever seen in my life.

I'm sitting on a rose-shaped chair with Frog Strips on my lap, stroking her back as she bobs her head side to side. Mortician wouldn't let her tattoo his ass, but he said she could put a small one on the back of his hip. We don't have any tattoo guns around here so Nan is giving him a homemade one.

I've never heard of anyone doing it this way. The process looks pretty painful. Nan is dipping a sewing needle into ink from a broken pen and jack-stabbing Mort in the hip flab with it. His face is a silent shriek as she works on him like a piece of wood, spit-wiping blood and black-drip, creating a dotted "A" with a sloppy circle around it the size of a half dollar.

When she is finished it looks like a swollen connect-the-dots drawing created by a three-year-old. But it is recognizable as an anarchy tattoo.

"You can't get more punk than a home-made tattoo," Nan says.

She's right about that. It says right

here on page 52 of the idiot's guide:

SLOPPINESS = PUNK.

Mort washes his hip with Nan's old tea. I offer him a metal bowl so he can see the tattoo in the reflection, but he just shakes his head at it.

"I'm telling you," I say, "you've gone through all of that for nothing. It's just going to wash off."

"I wish it would wash off," he says.

"It'll probably scab up a little," I say, "but once it heals there will be nothing left of it at all."

☺

Two days of babysitting the newcomers and waiting for the tattoo to fade away from Mort's hip.

"I told you," Nan says.

"It'll come off, I swear," I say.

A couple more days pass. They complain about eating sardines every day. Frog Strips is avoiding Breakfast like he's made of hot lava.

Another day. I examine the tattoo. It is healing, but the ink is still there. We have tried scrubbing it off, but it isn't going anywhere.

☺

"Now do you believe us?" Nan asks.

I shake my head.

"It's not permanent," I say. "Just give it a few days and it will clean off."

☺

A few more days.

"Now do you believe us?" Nan asks.

I don't know what to say. The scabs have healed but the ink is still dark.

"It's really staying . . ." I say, eyes roll-wandering Mort's hip.

"Make me a citizen already," Mort says.

I shake my head at him and sigh, avoiding eye contact.

"What?" he says. "This is a true anarchy tattoo, which means I get 50 extra points. Bringing my total up to 115."

I clean old sardine bones from a lunch tray and speak under my breath, "But tattoos you get after you die don't count."

Nan stomps her foot. "But we haven't died yet!"

"I don't know what to do," I say, and leave the room.

☺

An evening of quiet by the fire. The snow storm is still going, hitting hard against the windows and driving Breakfast into short bursts of spasm. Mort and Nan play with a deck of cards they found in an old footlocker, drinking hot clove tea.

"We'll leave in the morning," I say.

They don't look up.

"To where?" Nan asks.

"We have to go to Mosh City, the capital of Punk Land. The Punk Council is there. If you really are alive they'll know what to do."

"Mosh City?" Mort asks. "The punk guide

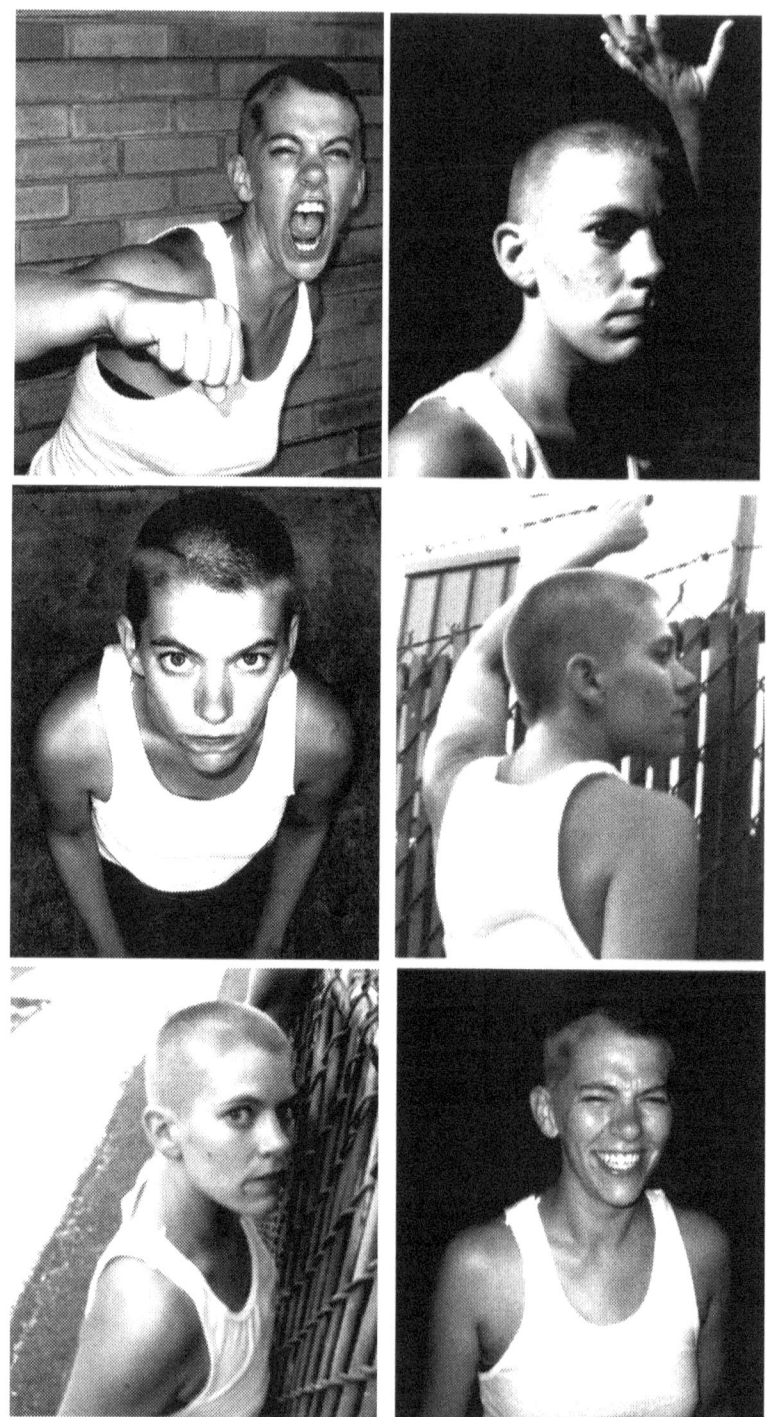

Photos of Nan in Rippington, New Canada

said that Pig Slut is the capital of Punk Land."

"They haven't updated the guide in a while," I say. "The Punk Council named Mosh City the new capital because it is a much larger and newer city. And a lot more punk."

"Does the Punk Council have that much power?" Nan asks.

"They control all of Punk Land," I say.

"They sound like Nazis," Nan says.

"Oh no," I say. "They might seem that way to you, but it's just because you're newcomers. The Council was put into power to make sure our world stays 100% anarchy."

Scene Five
Knife-Textured Crocodiles

☺

We bundle ourselves up and leave for Mosh City. Nan and Mort groan at me every time I say the city's name.

"It has to be the stupidest name ever," Mort says.

Snow is on the ground but it is no longer falling, a frosty wind against our numb ears.

"Wasn't there a band called Mosh City?" Nan asks, keeping Breakfast warm under her shirt.

Frog Strips is wobbling out of my backpack, her mouth opens and closes like a winking eye at Nan's lump of Breakfast under her tiny breasts. I don't remember if I mentioned this or not but dildos don't have any eyes or ears. They can only taste. They can find their way around by tasting the air. The pee hole just above the mouth is not really a hole and has no apparent function. It is just for show. Nothing squirts out of it or anything.

Sometimes I wish laser beams would shoot out of Frog Strips' pee hole, but nothing, not even grape jelly, ever comes

THINGS I WISH WOULD SHOOT
FROM FROG STRIPS' PEEHOLE

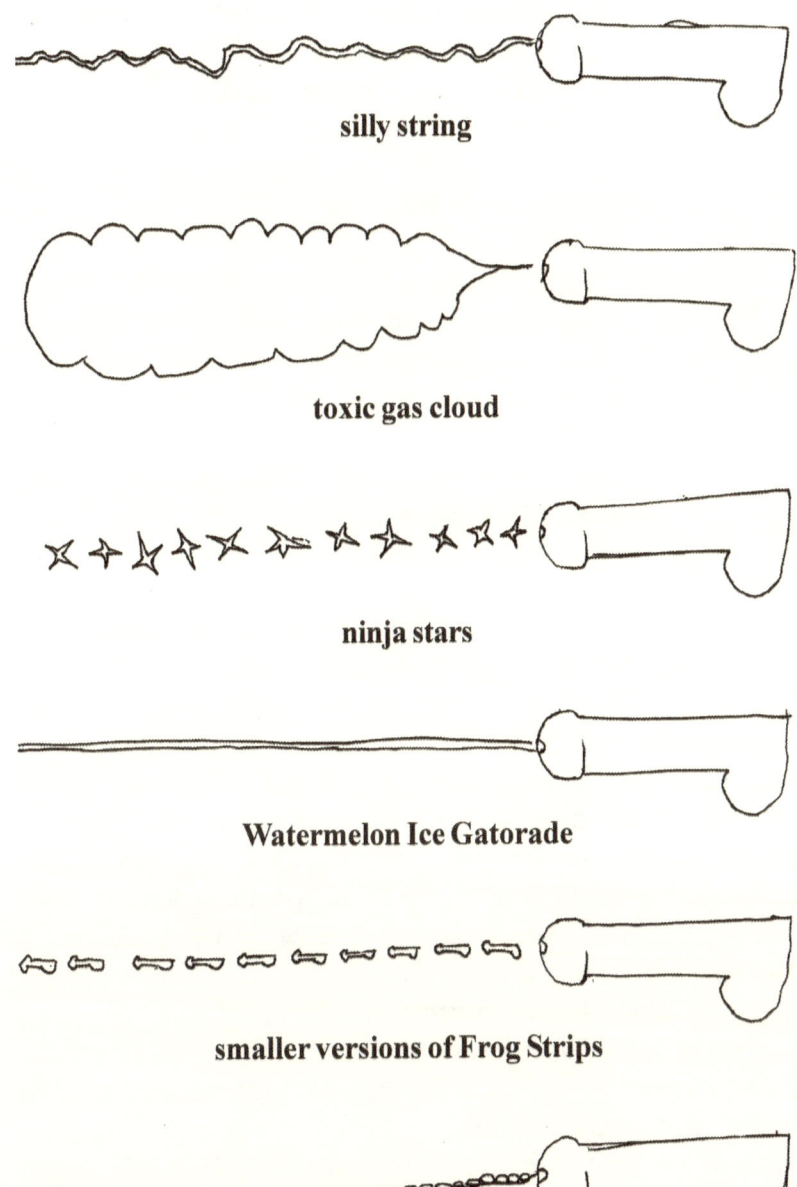

silly string

toxic gas cloud

ninja stars

Watermelon Ice Gatorade

smaller versions of Frog Strips

hooked chains
(like the ones in Hellraiser)

out of there. If she had lasers I would use
her as a Star Trek weapon whenever I was in
one of those moods. Not to hurt anyone or
anything, but because it would make me
more popular with the punk kids.
    Because, if you didn't know:

STAR TREK = PUNK.

    Well, not according to the Punk Coun-
cil, but the guy with the dreadlocks who
let me into Punk Land told me so. He saw
that I was wearing a homemade federation
pin and said that showing someone the Vulcan
sign is probably the punkest/toughest thing
you can ever do, ever.

    ☺

    The guy who let me into Punk Land was
named Tomax and he was not really all that
punk. He didn't have any spikes or a mohawk
or weird-colored hair or a jacket coated
in punk band patches and pins. He was just
an Italian skater with dungeons and drag-
ons figurines on his desk. Yet he was considered an authority on punk. This was
before the Punk Council, however, and as I
said, things were different then. There
wasn't really a government or laws at all
besides the word of Sid Vicious. His word,
of course, was *anarchy*. So government and
laws did not exist.
    The guards at the gates of Punk Land
were all volunteers. It was a self-gov-
erned institution created by a group of
people who wanted to keep the fascists,

the Christians, the corporate monkeys, the consumer whores, and the conservatives completely out of Punk Land. They were friends of Sid and knew exactly who to let in and who not to let in. But after the Punk Council was formed, the institution was completely revised. People like Tomax were replaced by those who had memorized The Complete Idiot's Guide to Punk, like me. When I got a 100% on the punkitude exam, which was the new way to get a job as a guard (and lucky for me I'm great at memorizing texts), the representative from The Council said I was truly punk rock.

The Council Rep was wearing a button-up short-sleeved white shirt and black tie, but with a mohawk and tattoos and eyebrow rings. He was kind of like a punk version of a Mormon.

☺

"Do we have to *walk* all the way to the capital?" Mort asks. "People drive cars here, don't they?"

"Of course there's cars," Nan says. "The road is paved."

"Nobody owns cars here, driving isn't punk," I say. "We'll catch the bus in Noid."

☺

The Complete Idiot's Guide to Being Punk is mostly several pages that state things that are punk and things that are not punk. For instance, *driving* isn't punk. Only public transportation is punk. Though Tomax told me—before he was fired and moved far away—that old Brady Bunch station wagons are very punk to drive, almost as punk as wiener mobiles.

Some things that are punk:

Mr. T is punk.
Spam is punk.
80's sitcoms are punk.
Midgets are punk.
The hamburglar is punk.
Super-8 movies are punk.
Martians are punk.
A meatball sub is punk.
Jews are punk.
Casino carpeting is punk.
Gil Gerard is punk.
Bongzilla is punk.
Sporks are punk.
Peanut brittle is punk.
"Manimal" is punk.
Chloraseptic spray is punk.
Ulysses S. Grant is punk.
TV dinners are punk.
Brain cannons are punk.
Neil Hamburger is punk.
The game 'butts up' is punk.
Duct tape clothing is punk.
Lunch is punk.
Bootsy Collins is punk.
A Sneed is punk.
The blob is punk.

I don't really understand why these things are punk, even though the book has short descriptions that are supposed to explain everything.

Passages from The Complete Idiot's Guide to Being Punk:

#398 - Ulysses S. Grant.
Ulysses S. Grant was a BIG fat guy with a beard who was drunk all the time and became President for some reason.

In other words:
ULYSSES S. GRANT = PUNK.

#2769 - Botulism.
Eating food out of garbage cans proves you are tough and shit, especially if it makes you sick and you die.

In other words: BOTULISM = PUNK.

#22 - Ninjas.
A ninja can waste you with a sword and breakdance your ass into the dirt.

In other words: NINJAS = PUNK.

I still don't understand why these things are punk. I didn't even know that ninjas can breakdance.

The list of things that are not punk are even more perplexing.

Some things that are not punk:

Clocks are not punk.
Eggs are not punk.
Mork from Ork is not punk.
Smoking liquid plummer isn't punk.
"Santa with Muscles" isn't punk.
Mr. Miagi isn't punk.
The urban dictionary isn't punk.
Sporks are not punk.
Sonic The Hedgehog is not punk.
A cop mustache is not punk.
Wil Wheaton is not punk.
Athletic champions are not punk.
The word 'whiff' is not punk.
Grammar is not punk.
Gang of Four is not punk.
Pizza magnets are not punk.
Spelling cool 'kewl' is not punk.
Hamburger Helper isn't punk.
Outer space is not punk.
Tom Hanks is not punk.
Fraggles are totally not punk.
Dancing tango isn't punk.
Being an elf isn't punk.
Candy corn isn't punk.

An example:

#87872 - Eggs.
Eggs are white, ovalish things that
come out of chicken's butts and taste like
crap when you eat them.

In other words: EGGS = STUPID.

So this means eggs aren't punk just
because the author of The Guide doesn't
like them? Or is there something more to it
than that? It is a mystery. Just like the
mystery of why *sporks* are listed in The
Guide as being both punk and not punk, for
the exact same reason.

Check it out:

#837 - Sporks.
Sporks are plastic spoon/fork hybrids
that can be found in school cafeterias,
food courts, and homes for the elderly.

In other words: SPORKS = PUNK.

#5278 - Sporks.
Sporks are plastic spoon/fork hybrids
that can be found in school cafeterias,
food courts, and homes for the elderly.

In other words: SPORKS = STUPID.

☺
They used to update the Punk Guide
every month, but I haven't received a new

copy in a year, probably because the punk
mail doesn't reach as far as the gates
anymore.

They update the guide because punk is
a trend and trendiness changes constantly.
Some things are considered punk one year
and then the opposite of punk the next.
Every so often, a guy from the Punk Council
will address Mosh City on top of a graf-
fiti-caked balcony. He or she (usually he)
will say something like, "I declare goose
feather pillows are now the hip new punk
rock things to own, they have replaced
corn muffins. So go get rid of your corn
muffins and pick up some goose feather
pillows right now unless you want to be
complete losers."

I'm probably very far behind the times
now, but that's okay. I'll be able to memorize the new edition of The Guide within a
week. I just feel bad for never mentioning
this to Nan and Mort, who I've been forcing
to study my one-year-out-of-date version
of The Guide.

☺

Nan and Mortician agree with some of
the passages of The Guide (such as Mr. T
and the blob and midgets) but do not like
to admit it.

They say, "Creating a guide to punk is
probably the most anti-punk thing you can
ever do."

"Are you saying Johnny Rotten isn't
punk?" I ask.

"Oh yeah," Nan says. "He wrote that

thing, didn't he?"

"Yes," I say. "And he's one of the punkest people in this place. I mean, he was the front man for the Sex Pistols!"

"I don't care," Nan says. "If he wrote a guide to punk then he's totally gay."

"You don't know what you're talking about," I say. "After you've been here for awhile you'll begin to understand."

☺

There are knife-textured crocodiles crawling through the woods along the road.

"What the hell are those?" I ask, throwing myself down behind a heap of brown ice.

"They must have come from the walm," Nan says, looking down at me in the mud.

"I thought you said you destroyed the walm," I say.

"It's been around for months, perhaps years, before we came through," she says. "Who knows how many creatures have made it into Punk Land since then."

"Are they dangerous?" I ask.

"Probably," she says. "But at least they aren't scorpion flies."

☺

When we get to Noid, there a moun-tainous stone wall in front of the town, blocking our path.

There are skinhead corpses lying in the road. It looks like a punk rock battle took place here. A circus-mist rises out of the woods.

"What happened?" Nan asks. Breakfast wants to know, too.

"It's a mystery," I say.

Nan asks one of the corpses.

The corpse says, "Can't talk. Dead."

☺

"I've been out of touch for a long time," I tell them. "Things have changed."

The two semi-punks frown at me.

"Let's follow the wall," I say. "There's got to be a way in here somewhere."

BEING AN ELF ISN'T PUNK

Scene Six
Baby Underground

☺

We walk around the wall, stumbling over more skinhead corpses until we get to a dirt road leading to a gate.

"It's like the middle ages," Nan says.

"Everything is primitive on this side of Punk Land," I say.

I ring the bell a few times, my eyes on a pile of corpses trying to adjust to a more comfortable position. There are large bullet holes in their muscled shirtless chests.

A guard with a cactus handlebar mustache peeks out of a barred window and grunts at a sandwich. "Yeah? Who are yous, there?"

By the way:
HANDLEBAR MUSTACHE = FUCKING AWESOME.

I tell Mort and Nan I'll do the talking.

"I'm a clerk from the gatehouse," I say.

"What gatehouse?" he spits.

"The one by the gate," I say. "Of Punk

Land."

"Yeah, but there ain't nobody there no more."

"I was the only one left," I say. "Nobody gave me orders to leave so I kept manning the post. I've been alone for months."

"Yeah, well we don't like no Council supporters, there," he says.

"Council supporters?" I say. "Look, I don't know what is going on around here. I've been out of touch for a long time."

"Look, unless yous knows somebody in here who'd be willing to vouch for ya I can't let ya in."

"I know a few people," I say. "Is there a guy named Grak? Or how about Tomax?"

"We ain't got no Grak in here," the guard says. "There was a Tomax but he's not here no more, so he can't vouch for yous."

I race through my head for somebody who might know who I am. I've never been very social. I guess I can try my band members, but I don't remember most of their names.

I say, "How about Flash, Breaker, or Zap?"

"No," the man says through his mustache.

I frown at him, but then realize those might have just been imaginary friends of mine and not the members of my band. I try to remember the drummer's name, who was Grak's friend, who I went to a bar with one time.

"How about Teeko?"

Outside of Noid there is a flag with this picture on it:

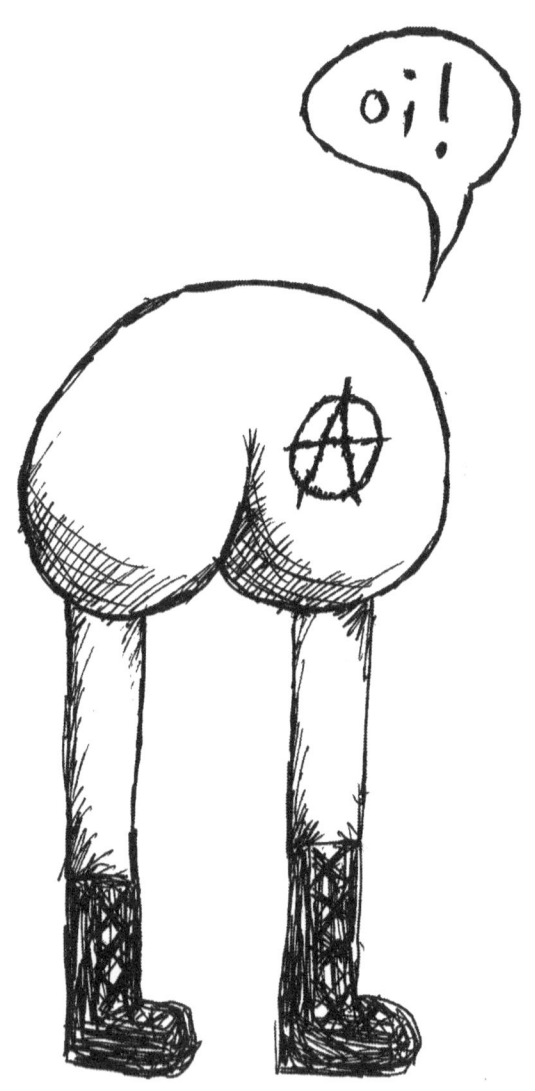

"Oh, Teeko, yeah there's a Teeko. Lives on my block. He might be the guy. What's your name? I'll send for him."

"Goblin," I say.

☺

Teeko was Grak's best friend, even though I liked to pretend that I was Grak's best friend. He was a Mr. T drummer but was more of a butt rocker than a punk, but I guess there wasn't a Butt Rocker Land for him to go to.

He was in my band with Grak and two other guys that I don't remember and we were called THE GLASS EYES.

The Council made it mandatory for every person in Punk Land to be a member of a band, even if you couldn't play an instrument. The band is supposed to be like your family in every way, and every family is recorded at the totally punk registrar's office. And once in a band, it is permanent, just like a family.

The Glass Eyes never played a show. I don't know who came up with the band name but I'm sure it was just a quick decision made by just one or two of us. Only Teeko knew how to play an instrument, so we weren't planning on The Glass Eyes being a real band. We just did it because we had to and if we didn't choose our family/band then somebody else would have done it for us.

I've heard about what they do with people who aren't in a band. They usually round up about fifty bandless people at a time and put them in a large room. And none of them are allowed to leave until they've joined together into groups.

These forced-bands have never worked out. Some of them have a few assihol drinks together from time to time but never create any music, while others dissipate immediately after forming. Even though they have failed in creating new performing-bands 99.9% of the time, The Council insists on continuing this.

"All punks should want to be in a band," The Council says.

☺

I remember one time when a group of people were put into the forced-band room, they all joined together to form one large 50-person band.

And they called themselves:
BEING IN A BAND IS GAY.

☺

The mustachioed guard comes back an hour later with Teeko who looks to be about twenty years older than I remembered. A brown leather jacket and ragged hair.

"Yous shoulda told me you're in his band, there," says the guard, opening the gate for us. He doesn't question Nan or Mort. "I could've just scanned your barcode."

"Barcode?" I ask, approaching Teeko who has a huge smile on his face. I forgot about how he always looks permanently stoned.

"He's been out of touch, Clob," Teeko says to the guard. "He doesn't know about the barcode system."

"Barcode system?" I ask.

Teeko shakes his head. "Come on, there's a lot you should know."

☺

Upon entering Noid, the atmosphere goes from peaceful nature sounds to blisteringly loud Oi! music attacking from twenty different directions.

"Now *this* is Punk Land!" Nan says.

The city is much different than it was just a year ago. It has become a giant mosh pit. Skinheads and punks running through the streets punching and slamming each other. Oi! bands are playing everywhere and it's sometimes hard to distinguish between the band members and the audience. Perhaps half of the crowd are bands.

"Follow me," Teeko screams into my ear.

He moshes us through the street, running into deformed punks, skinheads, a half naked bald chick who hits me in the ear with a spiked glove, tripping over pretending-to-be-dead people, trying to keep Frog Strips from falling out of my backpack.

These kinds of cities are why I live at the gates of Punk Land. I get far too overwhelmed in these thrashing crowds and insane collages of music that attack my ears like bees from every angle.

Most of the buildings near the center of Noid seem to have been torn down by a tornado. The mosh pit is so large in that

DRAGON WARRIOR = PUNK

area that I would not be surprised if the moshing created a kind of people-tornado that flattened everything in its path.

And everyone is yelling, "Oi! Oi! Oi! Punk Rock and shit!" and shit.

Near the outskirts of town there is a suburb that is still noisy and pretty trashed but much more peaceful in comparison. There isn't any moshing and the music comes from cd players rather than live bands, besides a few practicing inside of garages and living rooms.

People are hanging out on their dead lawns, drinking Oi! brand assihol beers and pissing on the dead/asleep people in the gutters.

"It's not like the middle ages on this side of the wall," Nan says. "This is more like my definition of a punk heaven."

"Things have changed," Teeko says, approaching one of the houses. "Let's go inside."

A large skinhead barrels out of the house as we are entering, smashing us all aside like bowling pins.

☺

There are all kinds of different skinheads. Not just the neo-Nazis that the media used to exploit on TV, creating a lot of undeserved negativity to even the most anti-racist of skins.

I didn't know anything about them before I died, but I do now. Skinheads actually started as a subculture in the late 60's, which was made up of working class twenty-somethings who decided that being working class is something to be proud of. And the rich upper class is something to revolt against. They wore boots and bracers because it was their work uniform. And they shaved their heads so they wouldn't get lice.

A large portion of the skinheads were not white. Many were black and/or Jamaican. They listened to ska music and eventually Skinhead Reggae.

Of course, they were still violent. Working shitty jobs will get you pissed off enough at the world to start random fights for very little reason. Like the football hooligans, who would start fights with people who cheer for the wrong team.

But times changed. A lot of the black skinheads started growing dreadlocks and listening to Dub, which most of the white skinheads did not like very much. And the skinhead culture started moving in separate directions. Some years later, 2-tone was invented as a revival of skinhead reggae mixed with punk, and so 2-tone skinheads were born. And around the same time, Oi! was being invented as a more extreme version of punk that shared many of the working class ideals of the traditional skinheads. And then came the Nazi skinheads, who were mostly football hooligans recruited by the underground British Nazi Alliance. It was easy to create racists out of them after cheap laborers started pouring in from the middle-east, taking many of their jobs.

The evolution of skinheads and Oi! continued in these different directions for a very long time and it has been hard to tell any of them apart, especially in the United States. There of course came the S.H.A.R.P.s (skinheads against racial prejudice) and even subcultures of communist skinheads, goth skinheads, and gay skinheads. Of course, there's always the hate-everything skinheads and punks who take on the skinhead fashion style but not any of the traditional ideals (punks traditionally refuse to work).

There's also skinheads who aren't racist but still listen to Nazi Oi! because they are into violent music and think there's nothing more violent than hate-fueled Oi! but you have to be either a really open-minded person or a closet racist or somebody with a really really dark sense of humor to not become extremely offended by the lyrics. These types of skinheads, who don't have a name, tend to like the band Anal Cunt.

Nazis weren't allowed in Punk Land because fascism is the complete opposite of punk. But there are still tons of Oi! skinheads, mostly residing in Noid and its neighboring towns, so they call this area the Oi! region of Punk Land.

But I assure you there aren't any sieg-heiling skinheads running around Noid, except for the occasional punk who treats Mein Kampf like a work of comedy.

A poster on Teeko's wall:

**BOUNTY HUNTERS ARE
TOUGHER THAN FUCK**

☺

Sitting on an old pawn shop couch with chips and beers and old corndogs. There's a group of people hanging out in the kitchen playing Asshole. Teeko doesn't know them but doesn't tell them to leave. It must be a common thing to treat other people's homes like public places.

Nan and Mort have been warned about the assihol in the beers, so they are taking it easy. If they really are alive, the assihol might kill them.

"Noid has declared independence," Teeko says. "The roads have been blocked off. We have completely isolated ourselves from the rest of Punk Land."

"Why?" I ask.

"The Council outlawed moshing," he says.

"They outlawed moshing in Mosh City?" Nan asks.

"Everywhere," Teeko says. "The Council has redefined punk so much that skinheads don't fit in anymore. And once they said that moshing is no longer punk, Noid declared independence. Only skinheads or skinhead supporters are allowed inside the walls."

He drinks a beer.

"What else has happened to Punk Land?" I say. "I've been out of touch for a long time."

"It's hard to say," he says. "Things change every day in Mosh City, I hear. I don't even think it's called Mosh City anymore. We are almost as isolated as you were."

"What about the barcodes?" I ask.

"They put these in us so the dead can be identified without having to speak, and so their band can be contacted."

"That's a neat idea," I say.

I know that losing a member can be really devastating to bands who actually play shows. You can't replace a band member, so your band is unable to play shows until that person has regenerated back to life again.

"Unless you die anywhere near Mosh City," Teeko says. "Any corpse in a band with one or more skinhead members is considered a threat to punk rock. If found by Council loyalists, they are taken into Mosh City and are never heard from again."

"Why do they have to pretend to be dead?" Nan asks.

"You are new," I tell her. "You just don't understand."

☺

We stay in Noid for a few days before heading out to Mosh City, drinking and listening to a noisy band in Teeko's living room that plays just for us and the group of punks still playing Asshole in the kitchen (after three days!)

The only transportation left is the subway going to Happy Corpse, a neutral town that happens to be miles west of our target destination. But we'll be able to catch transportation to Mosh City from there.

"Do we have to go?" Mort asks. "I don't think I want to meet The Council. Let's just stay here."

"It's the only way," I tell him. "If I don't get your citizenships you won't be able to live anywhere in Punk Land. Not even the skinheads will let you stay."

☺

We say goodbye to Teeko and descend into the underground, where we can catch the train to Happy Corpse.

The underground is swarming with infants. We watch them through the plexiglass walls as we walk down the tunnel towards the subway. Piles of them fill the sewer system, crying and gurgling, crawling over each other. Some of them squish against the glass. An infestation worse than rats or cockroaches.

"Women still get pregnant here," I tell Nan. "But nobody grows old anymore. After the infants are born, they stay infants forever."

Nan stops and gazes at the filthy underworld of undead babies.

"There used to be nurseries for them at one time," I continue. "Or some people would keep their babies as pets. But most of them get thrown away. They toss them down into the sewers where they stay for all eternity."

"It's barbaric," Nan says.

I nod. The baby underground is huge here, much worse than I read about. I guess that's what happens after twenty years of births. Then I say, "I heard The Council found a way to clean up the baby under-ground, but I'm not sure how they do it."

Nan closes her eyes tight and holds in her stomach.

☺

Before boarding the subway, the at-tendant gives us a gritty look and tells us, "You know you won't be able to come back after you leave?"

I nod.

"Why's that?" Mortician asks.

"The Council will probably set up a blockade in Happy Corpse any day now. They want us completely isolated."

Mort and Nan give me worried faces and Frog Strips bites at Breakfast's finger-nails.

"No problem," I tell the attendant. I think I can live without Noid for a few centuries.

The attendant smirks.

"It's your eternity," he says.

As we board the train to Happy Corpse.

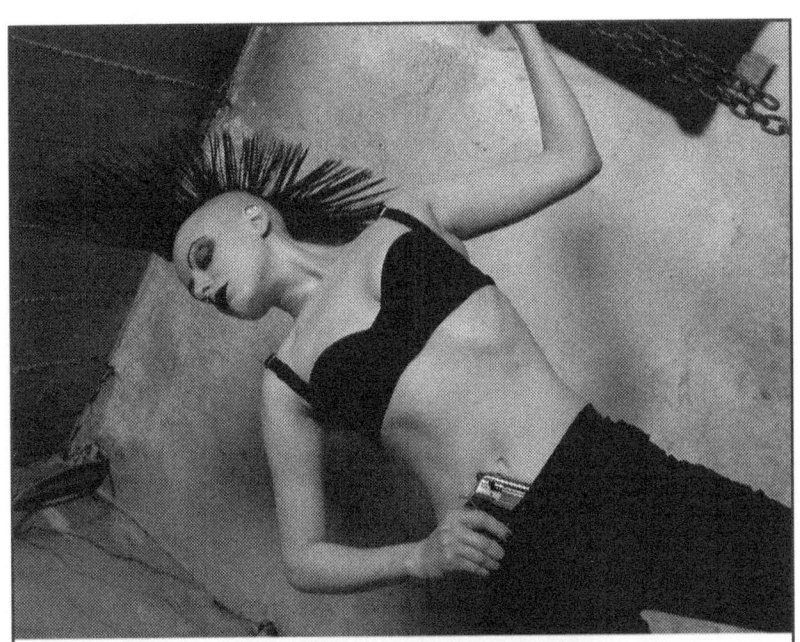

ACT TWO
THE HEART OF PUNK LAND

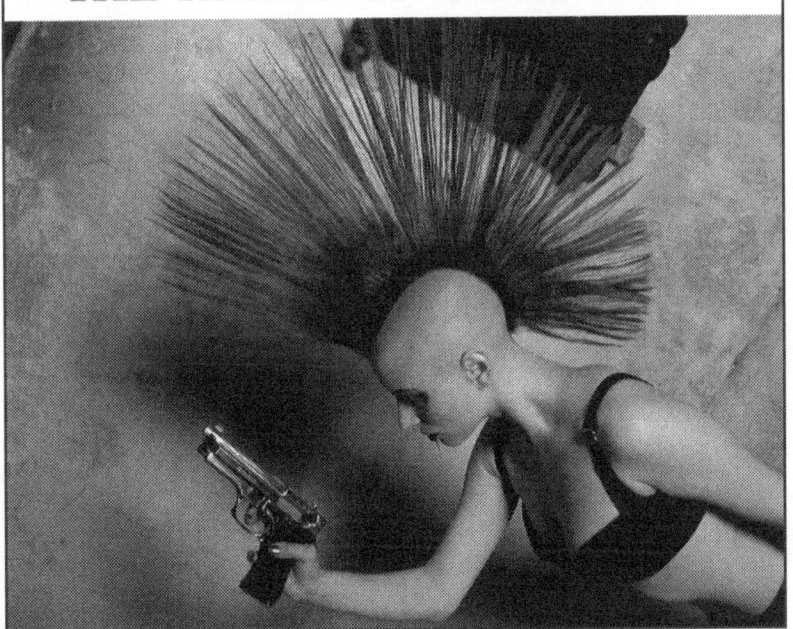

Scene Seven
Midget Olympics

☺

There's only the three of us on the subway, and perhaps a driver up there somewhere. Sitting on thick layers of icing graffiti, keeping silent like dead bugs on the windowsill.

I'm glad we are taking the subway instead of the bus. As I mentioned, I died by getting hit by a bus. And this is something I do not normally like to think about. Not because it was painful to die, but because Tekky, the love of my life next to Frog Strips, was the person who pushed me out in front of the bus.

Why she did it, I have no idea. We were kind of in love in our strange little way. She might have been weird, a little demented, but never violent. Not to me, at least.

But she was violent to bugs.

It really made her happy to step on insects with her boots or bare feet and say "squish!" Sometimes she would spend an entire afternoon dragging me around so I could watch her squash bugs under her feet. She liked to pretend to be some kind of giant and for some reason did the crushing in such a cartoonish way that was strangely cute.

Perhaps she watched so many cartoons that she thought that we lived in that cartoon reality. And that I wouldn't really die after being hit by a bus. I would just be a flattened pancake that would blink and walk around before accordioning back into a human being again.

Actually, her bug-squishing was like a fetish to her. Like her cutting fetish. Perhaps she wanted to see a human being crushed like a bug. If she had the power to shrink me down to finger-sized, I'm sure she would get a kick out of squishing me under her bare feet. But since that was impossible, maybe she wanted to see me squished by a bus.

That's the most likely explanation; she killed me to fulfill an erotic fantasy, to create a real life visual she could carry around in her mind to masturbate to.

I don't know what happened to Tekky after I died. I couldn't find her channel on my Heaven television, which means she must have died soon after my death. Perhaps she went to prison and was killed by somebody or herself. Perhaps she was so aroused by my death that she wanted to be crushed by some heavy machinery as well. She probably went to hell for killing me, which means she doesn't exist at all anymore. I believe that all of the souls in hell were wiped out, obliviated, as were the souls of Earth. Good thing the Lord doesn't have any authority over Punk Land or we would have been wiped out, too.

☺

We arrive in Happy Corpse in less than an hour.

They call it Happy Corpse because it was founded by an underground record label called Happy Corpse Records, which specializes in retard punk. Retard punk is very different than other punk genres because the band members refuse to learn how to play their instruments, the lyrics are utter stupidity, and they have no fans other than themselves.

Most of the retard punkers believe that stupidity, drunkenness, and being lazy and/or fat are the coolest things imaginable.

One interesting thing about retard punks is that they commonly follow trends because they think it is funny. Wearing a t-shirt of the lamest corporate band that nobody likes except hipster 12-year-olds is probably the funniest thing you can do in Happy Corpse. Which makes their position in Punk Land a very favorable one. The Punk Council thinks the citizens of Happy Corpse are good little trend-followers, but the underground punks know that the entire town is just incredibly sarcastic and actually making fun of The Council and their sellout bands.

The first retard punk we see in Happy Corpse is weaing a "Sister Act 2" t-shirt.

TOP 15 RETARD PUNK SONGS

"Your Muff Has Tusks" - Sockeye

"Jesus Gives Me Blue Balls" - That One Band

"Stinkin' Lincoln" - The Imperial Butt Wizards

"Big Chocolate Penis" - Sockeye

"Cheerios and Whiskey" - Cauliflower Ass and Bob

"Gatorade Suppository" - Hearseberry Taco

"Doogie Howser O.G." - That One Band

"Hearts of Metal" - Timwie Malmsteen's Rising Pants

"Super Duper Cripple" - Sockeye

"Sweater of Werewolf" - Breathilizor

"Pay-Per-View Metal Church Show" - The Don Knottzis

"Foreskin that looks like George Bush" - Boy In Love

"Tittyfuck a Coalminer" - Sockeye

"Snacks and Snacks and Snacks" - The Poops

"Grandma Used My Toothbrush as a Dildo Again"
- That One Band

☺

The mayor of Happy Corpse is the guitar player of the retard band called That One Band, which totally sucks and everyone hates them. His stage name is Johnny Thunderpants.

He had several other names, such as Timwie Malmsteen (as in: the king of all shredders) and Bob Backlund (as in: the misunderstood genius/pro-wrestler who wanted to become President of the United States) and a bunch of others because changing your name constantly is a punk thing to do. But Johnny Thunderpants is the one they put in the Happy Corpse tour guide, so that's the one he is most commonly called.

☺

Yes, Happy Corpse does have tourists. Quite a few actually. Especially around this time of year. Johnny Thunderpants created a month-long festival called the Midget Olympics, which doesn't have anything to do with midgets or The Olympics. Well, there are sports, but instead of the world's top athletes competing it's more like a bunch of fat drunk guys doing a bunch of stupid crap and then passing out.

☺

There is a menu of events posted on a flier board in the subway underground just before we enter the town. (There doesn't seem to be any babies in the underground here, maybe because the weirdo citizens of Happy Corpse are not sexually appealing to anyone).

Nan reads the event of today:

"The Cemetery Run?" she says.

"Oh yeah," I say. "That is one of their more popular events."

It was invented by the singer of That One Band, Trainstation Willy, who was completely obsessed with zombies, and so he created a zombie event where a bunch of drunk fat guys dress up like zombies run around in a cemetery until they pass out. Of course, there are no need for cemeteries in Punk Land, so Johnny Thunderpants had one built for the Midget Olympics. The challenging part of the event is that the fat drunk guys dressed up like zombies have to eat a bunch of human victims which are actually just huge piles of corndogs glued together with nacho cheese. Whoever passes out first is the winner.

The winner of all the events is whoever passes out first.

☺

"I want to check it out," Nan says. "These guys sound like my friends back home."

"We need to get going," I say. "We're farther away from Mosh City than we were in Noid, and we need to get you registered before somebody realizes you're not citizens and wants to throw you out."

"They won't throw us out," Nan says.

"Yes, they will," I say. "A couple years ago a bunch of Nu Metal guys scaled the wall into Punk Land and every single

The PBR
POGO JOUST

OBJECTIVE:

Four teams of drunk fat guys on pogo sticks will hop around attempting to knock down jousters on opposite teams. If you fall down or are knocked down you will be eliminated. The game is over once there is only one team left standing. Whoever passes out first is the winner.

RULES:

1) 5 cases of Pabst Blue Ribbon must be consumed by each team prior to the event.

2) Each team must have the combined weight of 1,000 lbs.

3) There can only be three people on each team.

4) Cheeseburgers are pretty good.

one of them was tracked down, beaten up, and kicked out."

Nan replies, "Yeah, but it doesn't seem like your government cares about who gets in or out these days. You were the only person guarding the gates."

"It's better to be safe," I say.

They grind their fists at me.

"Well, fine," I tell them. "The bus probably isn't leaving for a while anyway, so we can watch the Midget Olympics while we wait."

☺

After buying the bus tickets, we head through a crowd of punk tourists getting autographs from some local celebrity named Pig Champion and follow arrows to the cemetery. There are a couple of bands playing drunken uncoordinated song-like things with instruments that are not really instruments, but baby toys and kitchen appliances.

The crowd is pretty large for such a small town, but we manage to find ourselves some seats up close to the cemetery gates. The place is like one of those renaissance festivals, but instead of knights battling with blunt swords we'll be seeing fat drunk guys running around, puking. The cemetery is very cheaply constructed. The graves are pretty much just spray-painted cardboard boxes with the word "grave" written on each of the headstones. I guess the citizens are far too drunk and lazy all the time to create an authentic-looking graveyard. Or perhaps they think crappiness is way more Mr. T than realism.

☺

A large guy with a t-shirt that reads 'mullet.' is walking to a small stage in front of us.

I believe the guy is the mayor, Johnny Thunderpants. He goes to a microphone and clears his throat.

He says in a monotonic voice, "We have a very special guest who has pleasantly surprised us with a visit to our quaint little town . . ." A pause like he is turning a page in his brain. "Will you please rise for the leader of the entire world . . . Johnny Rotten."

The crowd stands and everyone looks at a group of men in business suits walking into the audience to find their seats.

In the middle of the crowd is an old punk guy who looks more like elderly rocker Rod Stewart than Johnny Rotten, but wears the same homemade-looking clothes that he did when fronting the Sex Pistols.

"When did Johnny Rotten become President?" Nan asks.

"This is news to me," I say. "The Council was formed to keep Punk Land government-free. There's not supposed to be any leader except for Sid Vicious."

The men in suits, who are probably Council members or at least work for The Council, lead the old Sex Pistols singer to a group of red seats in the front row just next to ours.

"Don't say anything," I tell them, as they cross in front of us and sit down.

The crowd, including the three of us, sit down with the suits and try not to look at them.

☺

I realize I am shaking. There is something deep down in me that is making me nervous, and I feel like I have to puke.

I believe retard punk bands usually play some sets before the Olympic events, but it seems that Johnny Thunderpants and his crew are far too nervous to let The Council hear their music. Complete stupidity is not punk rock according to the Punk Council, so they are probably trying to find a trend-following band to play instead.

☺

I soon realize that I am twitching frantically now, holding Frog Strips tightly in my hands.

"Oh shit," I say to myself.

I'm getting that primal urge to throw a dildo at someone.

Being in an audience watching someone on a stage just does that to me. I can't go to plays or concerts without getting the urge to throw a dildo.

But I realize my urge to throw Frog Strips is not aimed at Johnny Thunderpants over there. It is aimed at the person seated just a half dozen seats over:

Johnny Rotten.

☺

I close my eyes and concentrate, blocking all thoughts. If I can't stop myself from throwing my dildo (my poor Frog Strips) I can at least do it with my eyes closed and most likely miss my target.

I grind Frog Strips into my thigh, which doesn't seem to hurt the little girl, whispering to myself, "Don't you do it, don't you fucking dare."

I promised her I would never throw her at anyone ever again.

☺

I jerk out of my chair when a band starts playing.

My eyes open.

It is That One Band, Johnny Thunderpants' group, playing a noisy song called *Anarchy in the Ukrane*, with the singer screaming like a four-year-old girl and making farting noises on a trombone. The drummer flares his nostrils and makes a troll face at me.

The song doesn't really have anything to do with the Sex Pistols song, but it pisses Johnny Rotten off enough for him to get up and leave the show with his Council members following after him.

☺

The trend-following section of the crowd is in shock, so much that they nearly collapse after a dildo hits Johnny Rotten in the forehead.

☺

I didn't even realize I did it. My concentration had been broken and my subconscious took over, throwing poor Frog Strips at the punk President and hitting him square in the face as he looked back at That One Band to give one last scowl of disapproval.

But after the crowd realizes what has happened, the band stops, and everything goes silent. No noise at all. Not even the faint echoes of bands across town.

Then the members of That One Band begin to laugh. They have to put down their instruments to chuckle, and puke, and flip off Johnny Rotten as he stands there with a stupid look on his face. And all the Happy Corpse citizens join them in their banter.

That's when an army of policemen emerge from the background and swarm us.

"Police in Punk Land?" Nan asks, as the fascists race toward me.

They tackle me to the ground, and all I can see slamming into my face is a tin badge that reads:

Scene Eight
Shark Girl

☺
I awake in a small cell with a toilet for a pillow.

Not sure when I was knocked out. Must have been immediately after I was tackled by those cops.

Nan and Mortician are on the floor of the cell, still unconscious.

"I wouldn't try to stand up," I hear somebody say as I stand up.

My head swirls and I drop back to the ground, my stomach feels like it is popping when I vomit over the toilet. I notice a wound on my arm, a large gash that has been crudely stitched.

"I feel hungover," I throat-bubble at the voice.

"The Co-Po hit you with concentrated Assihol," says the voice.

My eyes find the source of the voice, lounging on the bed. A half-naked girl with demon-like eyes, nose ring, and a two-foot blue Mohawk, her Grinders hanging off the bed in my face.

"Co-Po?" I ask. "Council Police? When did they start a Council Police?"

She is carving an old turkey bone with her fingernails. "Where the hell are you from?"

"I've been isolated for almost a year," I say.

I rub the aches in my temples.

"You missed a pretty eventful year," she says.

"Yeah." I worm-groan.

Then I introduce myself.

Me: My name's Goblin.

Her: Hey, my name's Goblin too!

She said that very sarcastically, and is now going back to sharpening the bone with her nails. Not sure if she was serious or if that was supposed to be some kind of joke, or if she's bitter about something and wanted to make me feel stupid.

I'm feeling stupid.

I look out of the window but can only see a yellow and red wall.

"Are we still in Happy Corpse?" I ask.

She doesn't reply, busy carving.

I feel uncomfortable.

Some time passes and she says, "By the way, I'm going to cut off your head before the Co-Pos get a chance to."

I'm not sure if I heard her correctly.

"What?" I ask.

She doesn't reply, busy carving.

☺

A policeman opens the cell and curls a finger at me. He is a beefy guy with a buzz cut and a tattoo on his neck.

"Me?" I ask, looking back at the woman

on the bed who is deep in concentration.

The cop smug-smiles and curls his finger at me again.

I stand up, step over my friends' sleeping bodies, and approach. He begins to nod his head at me and opens an arm as if to embrace.

Keeping his half-smile facing me, he wraps one arm tightly around my shoulder, crushing my elbow into my ribs. And leads me down a hallway to a white door. Just before he sends me in, he presses his lips up to my ear.

"You are going to be put to sleep, you mutant fucker," he whispers.

☺

Inside the room, there is a small man in a black suit. Young but balding, with only a small fuzz of platinum hair, tattooed eyelids and lips. His eyes grilling against me.

"Sit down," he says, and diverts his eyes down to some paperwork.

I sit in a chair facing him.

He doesn't speak, busy writing words or maybe drawing a picture.

"Where is it?" I ask.

He raises a finger at me and continues his work.

A few minutes pass. My hands are shaking. Not sure if it is from nervousness or the hangover feelings.

He puts his pencil down and looks up at me.

I get a quick glance at his paper before he puts it in a file folder:

The man straightens his back and smooths his head Gestapo-like.

"My name is Tick-Tock," he says. "I am one of The Council Elite, as I'm sure you have already surmised."

I shrug.

"But we have no idea who you are," he says. "You have not had your badge installed."

"You mean the barcode?" I ask.

He just wrinkles his chin in response.

"Where is she?" I ask.

He blinks.

"You have really hit a nerve with us," he says. "We didn't know a threat like you existed until today. And we want to know if any more of you are out there."

I don't know what to say. His gaze makes me sink in my chair.

"I'm sorry," I tell him. "I didn't mean to throw the dildo at Johnny Rotten. I've got this disorder, you see. I didn't mean anything personal, I just get the urge to throw dildos at people from time to time."

"We dissected that . . . *thing*," he says. "It is an abomination."

I cry, "You dissected her! Frog Strips? I want to see her!"

"We couldn't kill it," he says, "which means the thing has an immortal soul. A dildo with a soul!"

He waves a fist at me for some reason.

"She came with me from Heaven," I say. "I'm so sorry I threw her at Johnny Rotten. But she is a living thing. Please, let her go. She has nothing to do with this."

"No," says Tick-Tock. "I'm not stupid. That thing is a weapon and you're going to tell me how it works."

"A weapon!" I say. "No, she's just a dildo."

I pause.

"Wait . . ." I say. "You don't think I was trying to assassinate Johnny Rotten, do you?"

"Well, weren't you?" he asks.

"Of course not! I have a unique mental disorder. I didn't mean any disrespect, and I for sure wasn't trying to kill anybody."

"You can stop lying," he says. "We know you are a spy."

He holds up a microchip in a plastic bag.

"We found this in your arm," he says.

I squint my eyes at it, and then rub the gash on my arm.

"What is that?" I ask, rubbing the wound.

He blinks.

"You're a spy sent from Heaven," he says. "And I'm sure you're not the only one."

"I've never seen that before in my life!" I say.

Words go spewing out of me: "My name is Goblin. I worked at the gatehouse for almost three years. I know I originally came from Heaven, but I threw a dildo at God, the same dildo, and got kicked out. I've always been loyal to Punk Land and The Council. I know several editions of the Punk Guide by heart. I'm not at all a spy."

He leans back in his chair and taps a pen on the table top.

☺

For hours I am interrogated but am just as confused and worried about the chip as they are. How the heck did that get in me? Was I purposely bugged by God Himself? Was I being used as a tool by Heaven

TICK-TOCK'S EYELID TATTOOS

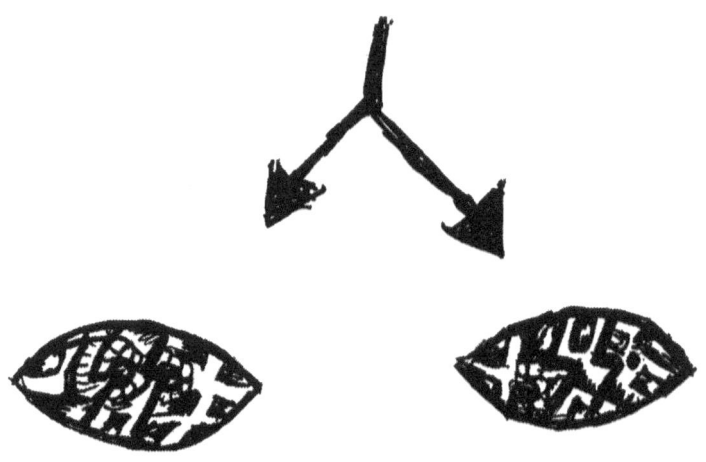

TICK-TOCK'S LIP TATTOOS

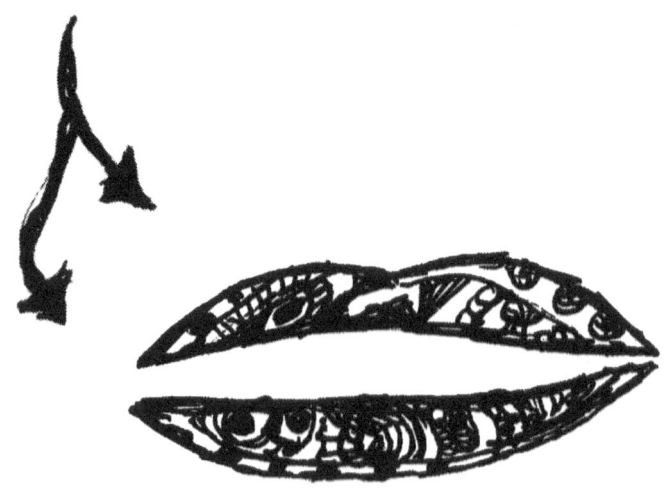

agents to spy on the people of Punk Land? Does Heaven have secret agents?

Tick-Tock isn't buying it. He is convinced I am some kind of operative and that my dildo stunt was some kind of assassination attempt against the punk rock President.

☺

I am placed in front of a window to watch the execution of Johnny Thunderpants, the now ex-mayor of Happy Corpse, and the rest of the members of That One Band.

"This is what we do to our enemies," Tick-Tock says, and I am beginning to feel like I have somehow been transported to some cheesy James Bond movie, only I look more like a hedgehog abortion than Sean Connery, and have no gadgetry at all.

They take the members of That One Band out in front of the town and line them up against a sheet of metal full of holes. It is like a giant cheese grater. No, I think it really *is* a giant cheese grater. The Council Police lift Johnny Thunderpants up in the air and grind his face into the metal.

Boil-shrieks rumble the town of Happy Corpse as the band is grated up into strips of flesh. The singer is grated feet-first so his girly screams can find a new pitch, and the drummer is grated ass-first.

I want turn away, but can't get myself to. My eyes frozen in morbid captivation.

"The best part is," Tick-Tock says, "we can keep shredding their parts over and over again without giving them a chance to regenerate."

I squeeze out some words, "But that is against the rules. You are supposed to pretend they are dead until they rejuvenate completely."

"Yes, that's right," he says. "We plan on pretending they are dead as we grate them into shreds, over and over again, perhaps for years."

He taps his thumbs on the back of my meat mohawk.

"And we'll do the same thing to you if you don't cooperate," he says.

☺

I am put back in the cell for a breather, still hangover-dizzy, and see that Nan and Mortician are awake, making friends with the punk girl who is still carving on the turkey bone. She must have fingernails of steel.

My body folds into the floor.

"They have Frog Strips," I say, lying in stickiness.

"Breakfast, too," Nan says.

She points at a cardboard box on an officer's desk.

"He said they dissected her," I say.

Nan pauses to feign sympathy.

"Breakfast isn't moving," she says, watching the box. "I don't know what they did to him."

Mort sits down on the bed between the punk girl and me.

"Did you meet Shark Girl?" he asks.

I look up at him and then her. Shark Girl? I examine her features and see that she does look like a shark girl. Her mohawk is like a fin.

"Yeah, we met," I say. "She said she wants to cut off my head."

Shark Girl stops her carving and eyes me with icy-penetration.

"You deserve it," she says.

☺

When Shark Girl is done with her carving, she shows it to Nan, who shows it to Mort, who shows it to me.

It is some kind of small knife made of bone. Sharp and intricately designed. A work of art.

This is what it looks like:

"We need to get their attention," the shark woman says.

And we nod at her.

☺

Mort is on the floor pretending to be sick. The rest of us scream for help, my throat raw and itchy. But none of the guards come.

"Let's forget it," I say. "It'll never work."

Nan points through the bars.

"Look!"

I turn to see Breakfast crawling on his fingers like a lightning-spider towards us.

And on his ring finger: keys.

☺

Nan sweeps Breakfast up into her arms and kisses each of his fingers.

"That's a pretty smart hand," Shark Girl says.

"It was my boyfriend's," Nan says with a BIG smile.

Scene Nine
Cripple Elvis

☺

We are in a Co-Po mobile racing out of town, covered in blood.

The shark girl killed three Council Policemen with the turkey bone knife she carved. It took seconds for her to slice their throats open, but the lousy pigs didn't lie down and pretend to die right away like they're supposed to. She had to stab them through the eyes and/or break their necks, leaving them blind, temporarily paralyzed, and screaming on the ground.

I always thought it would be hard to keep silent after an excruciatingly painful death. Glad it wasn't me.

Shark Girl has a well-deserved nickname. She moved like a fish in water when fighting, weaving through assihol bullets, and ripping flesh like a blender with only a single tooth. Just a minute went by and she had dropped three policemen and hot-wired one of the Council's automobiles, a white SUV, and got us all out of there.

"You're amazing!" Nan tells her. "What were you imprisoned for?"

"I was never imprisoned," she says.

I would ask the woman if she still plans on cutting off my head, but there is something caught in my throat.

I don't know if I'll ever see my beloved Frog Strips again.

☺

The Council Elite are the only people in Punk Land allowed to own cars and still be considered punk. Their car of choice is a white mini-SUV, the kind with that hip off-roading style but without four-wheel-drive.

Mortician finds a briefcase at his feet and makes paper airplanes out of the sales reports within.

"Where are we going?" Nan asks her new best friend.

"Scum Fuck," the woman says.

"Why there?" I ask. "There's nothing but gutter punks in that shit hole."

"That's where they told me to take you," she says.

☺

I'm beginning to forget about Frog Strips and worry more about myself. This Shark Girl wanted to cut off my head, and now she's saying that somebody told her to take me to Scum Fuck.

Who is she really? Or, a better question, who are the people who want me in Scum Fuck?

My head churgles when I brainstorm. No ideas.

This has to have something to do with the chip that was taken out of my arm. Perhaps they also believe I'm some agent from God's S.S. if there really is such a thing.

I stroke my thumb and pretend Frog Strips is with me, to comfort me.

☺

In a small town called *Wiloby* we stop for some lunch at the café where Elvis happens to be performing.

Elvis, who was once the King of Rock and Roll, isn't at all popular in Punk Land, but he was one of the original punks who left Heaven, and calls himself *the* original punk. I guess his reasoning is that punk is all about rebelling through music and I guess he was supposed to be the first rebel musician.

So as we sit at a table, The King is up on stage performing some new material which is really a bunch of bland variations of "I'm All Shook Up" that sound more like something Billy Ray Cyrus would come up with. And we are eating sandwiches, completely disinterested, as is the rest of his audience.

Elvis is still the overweight old Elvis that he was when he died, but is now extremely deformed. His deformities are so elephant/slug-like that he cannot walk on his natural legs anymore and has become wheelchair bound.

There's a banner on the wall behind him that reads:

He's such a pathetic sight up there, playing his acoustic guitar with a bubbly mutant arm to a crowd that hardly notices him, swinging his wheelchair like the wheels are his hips, and saying his popular catch phrase, "Thank you, thank you very much," at the end of each song, even though nobody claps for him.

It's too bad there wasn't a Rock & Roll Land for old Elvis to go to. He would have been the god of that heaven as Sid Vicious is the god of this one. He goes completely unappreciated here, yet he doesn't seem at all bitter or even apathetic about it.

Perhaps Cripple Elvis is the definition of punk.

☺

"I thought *Shark Girl* was just a cute nickname," Nan says, examining the punk woman eating a sandwich.

I see it too.

Her eyes . . . they roll back into her head when she takes a bite, revealing a shiny protective eyelid, just like sharks' eyes when they bite into prey.

She bites her sandwich again with a wide mouth and we see many rows of teeth. They are more like human teeth than shark teeth, but there are rows of them. I don't think she has any molars, either.

After she is done chewing, she says, "I never told you my name was *Shark Girl*. I don't really have a name. You introduced yourself as Nan, and I said, 'I'm a shark girl.'"

"Arrgh," Mortician says, "Are you half woman, half shark?"

"Something like that," she says.

"Do you urinate through your skin?" Nan asks with a BIG smile.

"No," she says.

"Do you breathe underwater?" Nan asks.

"No," she says.

"Then what good are you?" Nan asks.

"I'm like Spiderman, but a shark," she says.

ADVANTAGES OF BEING SHARK GIRL

Flexibility - Shark Girl's bones are made of cartilage, making her much more agile and light-weight. This is especially useful for doing compli-cated breakdancing maneuvers or kung fu acrobatics not unlike those per-formed by characters in the MTV ani-mated series, "Aeon Flux."

Heightened Senses - The eyes of Shark Girl are much like those of a cat. She can see through fog and in the dark. Her sense of smell is so keen that she can identify a person by their body odor from a mile away. This makes cheating on Shark Girl damn near impossible to get away with.

Extra Senses - Like a shark, she has the "Ampullae of Lorenzini" on the inside of her nose that allows her to "feel" electrical fields. She also has the shark's "lateral line" run-ning down her spine that helps her detect motion within the water, if she ever happens to be in the water. In Punk Land, Shark Girl is the ulti-mate champion of the game "Marco Polo."

DISADVANTAGES OF BEING SHARK GIRL

Urine Phobias - it is a common misconception that Shark Girl urinates through her skin. This is not at all true and yet people still assume that every time she sweats she is actually relieving herself, urine-soaking her skin, her clothes, and possibly another person (or persons) if she is partaking in an intimate situation.

Predatory Instinct - While living in a civilized society, Shark Girl must learn to control her urge to kill and eat anything that is smaller than her. Although this might be considered a strength in the cut-throat business world, it can only hurt her social life.

Child Rearing - Shark Girl spawns many children during the course of her lifetime. About a dozen offspring are born per pregnancy, which is far too many children for one woman to raise. And with her cold-blooded nature (not to mention the urinating through the skin thing) the father of her children probably won't stick around for too long.

Scene Ten
Mermaid-Flavored Bondage Museum

☺

Dreaming about Tekky:

We are like a couple again, strolling through the Sausage Zoo, holding hands, smiling at everything, squishing every bug we come across. I am happy, or think I am happy, so I pretend that stepping on locusts and ladybugs is a fun thing to do.

I buy her an ice cream and we sit down on a blue flesh bench, she orders me to keep her warm, and I keep her warm. My eyes divert from the meatloaf giraffe neck that is peering down on us, swarmed by flies.

"I have to ask you something," I say to Tekky.

She pinches my flesh Mohawk.

"Why did you kill me?" I ask.

She licks her ice cream at me.

"I've been haunted by the reason for a long time," I say.

"Oh, that," Tekky says. "I was just having fun."

"But you killed me," I say.

"I didn't mean anything by it," she says. "I was just flirting. Besides, if I didn't do it you wouldn't look as cool as you do now."

"I'm deformed!" I say.

"Yeah, it's neato," she says.

She touches my deformed parts.

"I love your spiky arms, swirly skin, and especially your meaty hair. It looks yummy!"

"I haven't forgiven you yet," I say.

"You can't stay mad at me," she says with icy lips, mashing a fly against my forehead.

☺

Waking up in Scum Fuck:

It is a town I have never visited. As a clerk at the gatehouse, I was supposed to be a fountain of knowledge to all new-arrivals, so The Council sent me to every major town in Punk Land to familiarize myself with them. So I could be kind of like a travel agent when I needed to be. But for some reason Scum Fuck was not one of the towns I was to visit, even though it is one of the largest cities.

The Council just said, "There's nothing but gutter punks in that shit hole."

☺

On Earth, gutter punks were either a type of dirty hippy or a type of dirty punk, depending on what region of the world you were in. The dirty hippy type are not the kind in Scum Fuck, though there are many hippies in Punk Land. Sometimes punk ideals and hippy ideals go hand-in-hand, especially with many 80's and 90's punks who embraced liberal views and vegetarian lifestyles. It's also not uncommon for hippies to have lots of piercings and tattoos, and not uncommon for punks to have dreadlocks or attend peace rallies. The only difference is that a lot of punks will beat the crap out of people who eat meat or disrespect the environment, whereas most-to-all hippies are pacifists. A lot of these types of punks are also straight edge and hate drugs even more than meat-eaters.

If you're ever smoking pot at an Earth Crisis show, you'll surely end up pissing off a lot of the straight-edge punks, who will then threaten you by crossing their wrists and saying, "Straight-edge in your face!"

But most punk gutter punks (aka squatter punks, aka street punks, aka scum fucks) have very little in common with the hippy gutter punks. They both enjoy being dirty, smelly, scummy members of an anti-society, but punk gutter punks have the full-on anarchy, fuck-you, destroy everything, traditional punk mindset that hippies completely abhor.

They usually believe that being homeless is the toughest most punk rock thing you can possibly do. And they don't give a shit about you or anything.

20 THINGS SCUM PUNKS FIND PUNK/TOUGH

1) Not taking showers.
2) Having crabs and/or herpes.
3) Eating out of garbage cans.
4) Drinking swill out of old beer bottles found behind dumpsters.
5) Smoking cigarette butts out of public ash-trays.
6) Sleeping on sidewalks.
7) Fucking on sidewalks.
8) Urinating on sidewalks.
9) Taking shits on sidewalks.
10) Sleeping and/or fucking on sidewalks covered in urine and/or shit.
11) Hopping trains.
12) Eating mountains of donuts that are thrown away every day at various bakeries and Dunkin' Donuts franchises.
13) Talking to crazy elderly people when at the homeless shelter.
14) Fighting for change. (If there's a nickel in the road, they'll waste you for it.)
15) Finding single girls with jobs who happen to think smelly punks are attractive, or are just incredibly lonely, who are willing to take them home and allow them to mooch for a few weeks.
16) Robbing all possessions from the women who take them home.
17) Pissing people off.
18) Using public transportation without paying for it.
19) Prostituting themselves for smack.
20) Just hanging out.

☺

Driving through Scum Fuck:

It is like a large city that has gone through a nuclear war, and only the gutter punks survived.

They are all lining the road, smashing things and setting everything on fire. Cum and shit stained pants.

A cockroach gets wasted.

They begin kicking our SUV and flipping us off as we drive through. Only a few of them realize we are not Council members. Or perhaps they all know we aren't Council Elite and attacking our SUV is just their way of welcoming us.

"It reminds me of home," Nan says.

☺

The dumpsters and garbage cans and public ashtrays are all replenished every three hours in Scum Fuck, through the divine powers of Sid Vicious. This keeps all of the gutter punks well provided for with all the essentials they need and have grown to love.

There used to be gutter punks all over Pig Slut and especially Mosh City, but The Council cleared them all out. They are only allowed in Scum Fuck and its outlining communities.

☺

The shark girl drives deep into the wreckage, roads spider in every direction but only one of them seems to be free of debris. The punks are growing in numbers and getting more violent, now throwing rocks or hitting us with bats. The windows crack into webs but do not break. Dozens of them spray-paint the SUV as they kick at the doors with worm-caked boots.

We turn on a small side road mostly free of debris, moving slowly through and giving the mucky punks a chance to really do some damage.

A few blocks down I see a rusted garage door creaking open for us. None of the street punks follow us inside.

☺

It is some kind of facility. Very clean. Open. Not a heap of ruins as it appears outside.

We travel through an empty parking lot, winding up a few levels, until we get to the top floor where the parking spaces are mostly full.

There are dozens of SUVs identical to ours. Instead of them being white, they are all mangled and caked with spray paint, dozens of colors, mud, dried shit and urine. No white showing at all. It's more like a punk junkyard than a parking lot.

We exit our SUV and examine the damage. It is now like a Jackson Pollock of spray paint and anarchy symbols.

There are a lot of sloppily written words like "Die!" and "Oi!" and "Fight!" as well as upside-down crosses and pentagrams.

Sometimes upside-down crosses and pentagrams are considered punk even though

they are commonly associated with Satanists
and the death metal crowd. I guess anything anti, including the anti-Christ, is
considered—

"Move your ass," the shark woman yells
at me, cutting off my thoughts and I realize I am still looking at the SUV as they
are waiting for me in the elevator.

"Oh yeah," I say and hustle over, meat
mohawk flapping.

☺

But as I was trying to say . . .

SATANISM = PUNK

☺

And speaking of death metal:

Death metal is pretty much the most
brutal/evil thing on the face of the planet.
Which is why it is so funny. The purpose of
a death metal band is to prove how much
more evil they can be compared to any other
death metal band. You have to constantly
top each other's evilness, as well as your
own evilness with each album.

Death metal has been around for such a
long time now that the bands have reached
such a high level of evilness/brutalness
that they are borderline stupid.

For instance: The band Deicide is in
the habit of creating new satanic symbols
which are pretty much just a combination
of a bunch of pentagrams and upside-down
crosses.

The first one they created was called a trifixion.

It looked kind of like this:

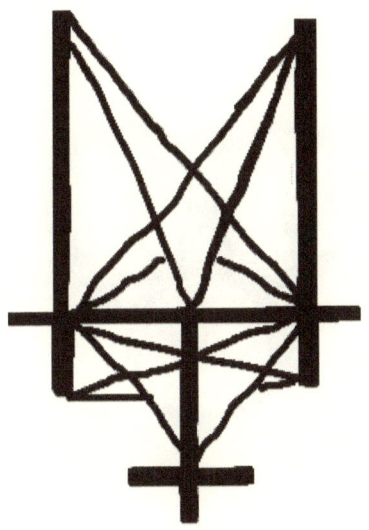

In response, the band Deth Corpse came up with their own totally brutal symbol, which looked like this:

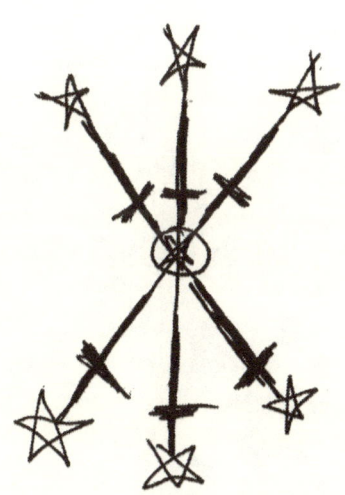

Several years later, Deicide created another symbol. Which was not very complex and pretty lame. I guess it's supposed to be three sixes or something.
It looked like this:

Finally, Deth Corpse created the symbol to end all symbols. It was the most evil yet the most retarded symbol the world has ever known.
It looked like this:

I don't know if there was ever a gay
death metal band. But if there was, I bet
their band symbol would be an upside-down
cross/penis.
Kind of like this:

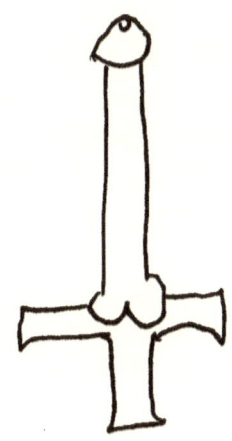

☺

After several minutes of elevators
and hiking through deserted branches of
the facility, we finally arrive at the
nerve center: a bustling office full of
smoking, drinking, scratchy music, and
people working at computers.
Some of the punks here are traditionally laden with spikes and motley hair.
Others dress rather conservatively, short
hair and pocket t-shirts and jeans. Others
dress in ways that I would not really call
punk, just weird. Like the guy with the
Zorro hat and disco sunglasses.

☺

We are taken past the offices to a mermaid bondage museum filled with several large aquariums containing live mermaids in underwater bondage displays. Nan takes a close look at one of them, staring through the glass and holding Breakfast like a teddy bear.

The mermaid has paper white skin and long green hair, green lips and eyes and eyebrows, and green pubic hair just above where her shiny scales begin. She is tied around a sunken treasure filled with golden skulls, arms tied to her fins, and wrapped through several loop-ring piercings that line her spine.

The mermaid looks at me and I feel something grip my nerves. I become aroused. Her eyes put me in a trance, make me hungry for her, even more than I was for Tekky when she would walk around my apartment topless, wearing only my underwear.

On closer inspection, the mermaid's white skin is almost translucent. I can see fluids moving inside of her. Blood rushing through her flesh. And the fishy smells don't seem to bother me as I step closer.

"Don't look her in the eyes," Tekky says, standing next to me in the place where Nan was standing.

"What are you doing here?" I ask Tekky, looking away from the fishy woman.

"That's how they lure their prey," Tekky says. "Look."

She puts my hand onto the glass and

the mermaid's mouth wrinkles open to reveal a blender of razor teeth.

"Humans are their food," she says.

☺

Nan snaps her finger at me and I drop out of the mermaid's trance.

"Come on," she says.

The others are waiting for me again. Tekky is not really here.

☺

We are locked inside a small boardroom decorated with razor wire roses. The shark girl doesn't tell us what we are doing here before she leaves.

"What is going on?" Mortician asks me.

Nan says, "They must be some kind of revolutionaries against The Council."

"I hate The Council," Mort says.

Breakfast bounces up and down at Mort.

"You don't have anything to worry about," I tell them. "It's me they want."

Scene Eleven
G. G. Allin

☺
 There are pens and paper so I'm able to doodle while waiting for the shark girl to return.

 I'm not really sure what to draw, so I draw this:

 It is a shark/missilelauncher.

☺

The room begins to fill. A river of people. Once all the boardroom chairs are filled, punks line up against the walls.

"Who are all these people?" Nan asks shark girl.

She responds with a frown.

The room continues to fill until every breath of air is spoken for. Like a packed bar.

We see many familiar faces. Famous punk icons from Earth. Ones that I didn't even realize had died. I recognize only the more popular faces, the ones who were on MTV that some punks consider sellouts (because it's never punk to make money for corporations), like the singer of Rancid and whatshisname from Green Day. I also recognize Gwen from No Doubt, who wasn't punk but still happens to be here for some reason.

The woman at the head of the table is their spokesperson. She introduces everyone in the room, mentioning which band they were/are from. All of them were supposed to have been in established punk bands before their deaths, which has earned them their office. The lower punks are not partaking in this meeting.

I don't recognize many-to-any of the names/bands of these people but I try to write them all down on my drawing paper so I can remember everyone.

This is my list:

Doc Corbin Dart of The Crucifucks, Danny Lore + Joe Koontz from Against All Authority, Paul Solger from The Fartz, Hoxton Tom of The 4-Skins, Mike McColgan of Dropkick Murphys, Doyle Wolfgang Von Frankenstein from The Misfits, Cretin + Anus + Spud from Dayglo Abortions, Mensi + Mond of The Angelic Upstarts, Ezra Riley of The Troma Kids, everyone from Rich Kids on LSD, Michiro Endo from The Stalin, Tony Kizmus of The Oppressed, Shahin Motia of Ex Models, B-face from The Queers, Rob McCulloch from Negative Approach, Tim Armstrong + Lars Frederiksen of Rancid, Nobby of Cockney Rejects, Atom from Atom and His Package, Al Schwitz + Dave Dictor from Millions of Dead Cops, Matt Hock of The Explosion, Steve Diggle of the Buzzcocks, Kat from The Spazzys, John Zorn, Keish from The Hard-Ons, L.G.Phillips of The Dickies, Peaches, Hot Carl + Warthog from Eat My Fuk, all the members of The Nerds, Hank Von Helvete + Rune Rebellion + Happy-Tom + Euroboy from Turbonegro, Stu Boy King of The Dictators, Jeff Morris of The Bruisers, and Richard Hell.

The spokesperson is named Kathleen Hanna, from the band Bikini Kill.

She tells us they have three leaders. Only one of the three is in the complex today. They are never in the same place at the same time, just in case one sect ever gets raided by Council Police.

The two not present are Henry Rollins, who I guess was a punk, he had a lot of tattoos anyway, and the other is named Seth Putnam. The one with us is the BIG bald guy sitting at the front of the table. He is the punk messiah, G. G. Allin.

Next to him is his brother, Merle Allin, who doesn't speak but has a really tough hairdo. I draw his portrait next to the shark/missilelauncher.

My picture of Merle Allin:

Hitler mustache

Lincoln beard

Then we introduce ourselves as Goblin, Mortician, and Nan Bradley.

The woman turns things over to their leader, G. G. Allin. His gruff voice is a bit muffled and he flares his nostrils with his words.

It seems he is reading from cue cards instead of coming up with the words on his own. He stares down at pieces of paper, and then looks up, then back at the paper. And everything he says sounds like something somebody else has written down for him.

He seems to be a bit burned out, hungover and bruised.

☺

G. G. Allin: (to Nan and Mort) Our gateway has been destroyed.

Mort: The Walm?

G. G. Allin: That gate allowed us to recruit new punks for the resistance. Ones that aren't brainwashed by The Council.

Nan: The Walm had to be destroyed. It would have sucked the life out of this world like it did to Earth.

G. G. Allin: We figured it was you.

Nan: Besides, there aren't any punks or any humans at all left on Earth. All their souls are dead.

G. G. Allin: We weren't looking for more Earth punks. We wanted the punks from the other dimensions. The creatures. They give us an edge.

Nan: Those creatures turned our home town, Rippinton, into a war zone.

G. G. Allin: Not all of them are that way. Most are civilized creatures, from societies similar to humans. And where there's a society, there's an anti-society. There are *punks*.

Nan: ?

G. G. Allin: We were collecting these creatures. Building an army. Until you made it difficult for us.

Mort: We didn't know . . .

G. G. Allin: We understand this. We understand you are not from Punk Land, that you are new. Not even dead yet. But since you destroyed the gateway, you'll have to rectify our losses.

Me: Us?

G. G. Allin: No, not you. The two living ones.

Nan: How do we do that?

G. G. Allin: You'll have to breed with the Blue-Violets.

Nan: ?

G. G. Allin: The shark people. We need to create more hybrids. (He points to the shark girl.) Like Six.

Pause.

Nan: (To the shark girl.) Is that your name? Six?

G. G. Allin: Six is the only of her kind here. She was born on Earth, after a Blue-Violet female mated with a human male and had a litter of human/shark hybrids. She came to Punk Land soon after her birth, when she was the size of a Barbie doll. Just three months ago.

Nan: How is that possible?

G. G. Allin: They mature at a tremendous speed. It took her only five weeks to grow to her current size.

Nan: But what about her mind? She couldn't have learned so much in three months.

G. G. Allin: It was passed to her through her genes. Blue-Violets are born with all the memories and knowledge of their parents. So Six knows everything her human father and Blue-Violet mother knew. She could speak both English and several Blue-Violet languages the moment her vocal chords were developed.

Nan: And you want to make more of them? You want us to fuck them and make an army of them?

G. G. Allin: You are the only living humans here. We are ghosts. We can't reproduce. Our children die at birth and forever haunt the underground.

Nan: But I'm already pregnant.

Pause.

G. G. Allin: That is not a problem. We can't use you anyway. You're female. It only works with a female Blue-Violet and male human.

Mort: Can I just masturbate into a cup?

G. G. Allin: No, that won't work. We have nine female Blue-Violets who have agreed to fuck you and donate their children to our cause. Within a couple months we can have more than a hundred hybrid assassins like Six. Human in appearance, but with the killing intensity of a shark. The Council doesn't stand a chance against us.

Pause.

G. G. Allin: We must return anarchy to Punk Land.

☺

Several days and I'm getting sick:

Mud-pickled in dark wet catacombs several miles underground, taken here by Six, the shark girl, who says she still wants to bite off my head. She's now using the term "bite" instead of "cut." And I have to stay down here until they are ready to talk to me.

The catacombs are vast and maze-like. A mile-long library of ancient corpses stacked like books up walls that stretch hundreds of feet into the prickly shadows. The bodies here are not real bodies. They were just taken from the imagination of Sid Vicious, like everything else in Punk Land. They seem more like bundled snail-piles growing out of the shelves.

I am all alone. Mort has been taken away so he can get raped by sharks, and Nan is in the medical station on the roof getting her fetus examined by a porcupine-faced doctor.

They have been sending food down a rusty pipe. Stale marshmallows and soupy corn muffins. But no water. I've been forced to drink out of the various puddles that collect from drips in the ceiling.

The water is full of disease, making me sick. I know I'll get back up again if the sickness or dehydration kills me, but I have not died in Punk Land yet and would prefer not to. Dying the first time was bad enough.

☺

"We're so far under ground," Tekky says. "Deeper than the place where babies go to be forgotten."

I'm sitting on a muggy log, leaning against a catacomb wall. My face just inches away from skeletal feet, sucking musty bones into my scabby lungs.

Not sure where Tekky came from. I woke from a trance to find her sitting beside me.

"When did you get here?" I ask her.

"I'm not really here," Tekky says.

"What, am I imagining you?" I ask.

"Yeah, I'm not really real," she says. "You're going crazy."

I touch her with my muddy toe. It doesn't go through her, her flesh is real, her muscled thigh is now smeared with mud from my toe. I don't seem to be hallucinating.

"Asshole," she says, spit-cleaning her olive skin.

Then she smiles. Her teeth glowing in the torchlight.

☺

A couple days with Tekky . . .

She claims to just be my imagination, but everything about her is real. She even eats my stale marshmallows when they come out of the pipe. She even takes craps in the sog-hairy section of the catacombs and sleeps curled up like a cat against my knee. Hallucinations don't normally do any of these things, do they?

It's just like the old days with her. Like we're back together again. I don't really say anything. I just watch and listen to her being her old hoppy/speedy self, drawing things on the walls and looking for bugs to squish.

All the drawings she does are the same as she did before. Fairies entering giant vaginas. After one particular drawing she says, "Looky, look, look!"

She takes me by the arm to see it, a very large fairy-drinking cunt drawing. It is the same as all the others, but for some reason Tekky acts as if this one is breaking new ground.

"Isn't it great?" she asks.

I nod at her.

"Look," she says, pointing at the little fairy in the picture. "This is you if you were to be shrunken down to fairy-size." Then she points to the giant vagina. "And this is my vagina."

Her smile grows huge at me. As if she has just asked me to marry her.

I don't make even a physical response.

"I like it," she says, and clucks her tongue. "I want you to be a fairy."

My throat is thick with itchy snot at her.

☺

Tekky leaves me while I'm asleep. Just as quickly as she came.

Leaving me with walls of drawings. Fairies and vaginas everywhere. And she took all the marshmallows with her.

☺

By the time the shark girl finally comes back to get me, I almost don't want to leave. I've gotten used to the place. The sickness in my head is gone and the water and food aren't all that bad. It's nice being alone and forgotten. Like I was before.

"We didn't forget about you," Six tells me in the darkness.

Helping me up and removing my filthy clothes from me. She walks me out of the catacombs naked and cold.

"It's been crazy up there," she says. "Things are finally starting to settle down."

"Are you going to kill me?" I ask.

"Only if we can't find a purpose for you," she says.

☺

Instead of washing my clothes and giving them back to me, they give me a new outfit: a leather uniform that is 90% bullet belts. I don't know how they did it but there are dozens of bullet belts wrapped around my torso, around my arms and legs, like a black metal mummy. I can hardly move with all the heavy bullets weighing me down and clogging my joints.

"I look like an idiot," I say to a mirror.

"That's how you're supposed to look," Six says, peeking over my shoulder.

☺

I'm placed in a room full of smashed

This picture is hanging on the wall:

televisions piled and nailed together into furniture.

The messiah's brother, Merle Allin, is in the room with me. Eating a nutroll and picking nougat out of his Hitler mustache.

I don't know if the Hitler mustache style has a name. People call it either the Chaplin or the Hitler. A trademark style for both fascist monsters and lovable tramps. But which is Merle Allin? Perhaps a combination of the two: A lovable fascist. Or perhaps he is just trying to piss people off. Nothing angers contemporary society quite like a Hitler mustache.

And, obviously:
PISSING PEOPLE OFF = PUNK

☺

We sit on television sets for chairs and stare at each other for a while. This guy is not very sociable and kind of awkward. Not as awkward as me, but still awkward. And awkward people just don't feel comfortable together.

He just chews his nutroll at me.

☺

Merle Allin: You didn't get your barcode.

Me: N-no, I don't know anything about the barcodes. I've been out of contact with the rest of civilization for most of the year.

Merle Allin: The Council issued

barcodes to strengthen their control. It started out as just a convenient ID system, much better than having to carry around a driver's license, but now it's become a dictator's wet dream.

Me: What do you mean?

Merle Allin: They now use the barcodes to keep tabs on the citizens. Most commonly to monitor punk points. These days people not only need punk points to get into Punk Land, but they need to maintain a level of punk to stay in. Points are awarded or taken away on a daily basis, depending on whether or not you abide by the standards written in the latest edition of the Complete Idiot's Guide to Being Punk. If your punkitude score goes below a certain level, you'll be escorted out of Punk Land.

Me: But I've never seen anyone getting escorted out of Punk Land. I was at the gate. Nobody's been there for months.

Merle Allin: We know. They haven't been escorting them out of Punk Land. They have been taking them underground. We're not sure where.

Me: Do you know why?

Merle Allin: No. We know very little about The Council. Not a single operative has been able to infiltrate them. All we know is that The Council did not come into Punk Land through the gates. They came through The Walm as your two friends did. They are not punks. They are soulless corporate fascists. Demons. Anti-punks. Somehow they overthrew Sid Vicious and then manipulated Johnny Rotten into being their lapdog.

Me: So Johnny Rotten isn't in control?

Merle Allin: He's been brainwashed. Possessed by corporate demons. He's not a target. We're trying to take The Council out of power and free Sid Vicious from whatever prison he's being held in. Once The Council falls, anarchy will be reinstated. And things will be as they're supposed to be. But it won't be easy. The Council is more organized than we are. More efficient. They know exactly what they're doing. We have only one edge.

Me: You mean Six? Those shark people?

Merle Allin: Not just the shark people. You.

Me: Me?

Merle Allin: They think you're a threat. They think you're an agent from Heaven. Obviously, you are not.

Me: How did you know I'm not?

Merle Allin: You passed the test. A real agent from Heaven would not have been able to last in the catacombs for so long. God's secret service is made up of only angels or souls who have lived in Heaven for hundreds of years. Either type cannot handle being in darkness for more than an hour. The eternal light of Heaven has made them extremely sensitive to the dark. You would have been smashing your eyeballs into your head on the first day if you were one of God's agents.

Me: You've met God's real agents before?

Merle Allin: Yes, there have been a couple. God has been spying on us since Punk Land was created. He's sent his angels in a couple times, but they're always spotted right away. Now he tends to place bugs on people like you, when unaware, just to monitor what's going on. It's not that huge of a deal. But The Council knows nothing of this. You have created a new threat for them, far more severe than the resistance.

Me: They think God wants to destroy Punk Land?

Merle Allin: Yes. God is a much more dangerous adversary than revolutionaries, so The Council Elite are going to focus all their efforts on finding you. We can use you to attract them away from our operations.

Me: Me?

Merle Allin: Six can take you to the outskirts of Punk Land. It is enormous, almost infinite, and mostly unpopulated. The Council doesn't have any power there. They'll never be able to find you. But they will try, and will need to divert most of their resources away from the capital to do so.

Me: Just me and Six?

Merle Allin: Six is all you need.

Me: But she said she wants to take my head off.

Merle Allin: She said that? She must like you. That's the way Blue-Violets flirt.

Me: By decapitating each other?

Merle Allin: No, just threatening to decapitate. You must have done something to impress her.

Me: All I did was throw Frog Strips at Johnny Rotten.

Merle Allin: Frog Strips?

Me: My pet dildo.

Merle Allin: Yeah, that is quite impressive.

Me: No, it was horrible. My poor Frog Strips! I need to get her back. The police took her from me. They think she's some kind of weapon.

Merle Allin: ?

Me: I know it sounds odd, but Frog Strips means the universe to me.

Merle Allin: If you agree to assist us, we promise to get your dildo back to you.

Me: I'll do anything to get back my Frog Strips.

Merle Allin: As soon as we overthrow The Council you will get it back for sure.

Me: She's just a baby.

Merle Allin: . . .

Scene Twelve
Pizza Cat

☺

They told me Nan's in the cafeteria so I decide to go for lunch. I could use some hot food.

In Punk Land, eating is much different than it was on Earth. For one thing, we don't need food to survive, but we get hunger and cravings. Sometimes our diet consists of stale marshmallows, oak leaves, dead bugs, paper, glue, pretty much anything that can fill our stomachs without killing us. Also, we don't have farms to produce food, so our food supply comes from the imagination of Sid Vicious.

But some of the time Sid's imagination is a little out there. An example is what we are eating for lunch today:

We are having pizza cats.

Pizza cats are small pizzas with legs. Not necessarily like cats, but they are small living things made entirely out of pizza. Their skin is cheese, their bones are bread, their blood is sauce, and they each have a variety of internal organs/toppings.

☺

In the cafeteria, there are punks killing and eating the wiggly pizza cats. Some slice up the cats to make them look more like food and less like living things, but others just eat them whole, taking bites out of their gut while they squirm in their hands.

I see Nan with her pizza cat, staring at it like a television on the table.

"Not hungry?" I ask, sitting next to her with piles of bullet belts and corpse smells.

"I don't think I'll ever be hungry again," Nan says.

☺

She lets me eat her cat, but only after I squish it into a gooey pancake. I normally would not eat a pizza cat either, but I haven't had hot food for a long time. The best thing about pizza cats is that their body temperature keeps the pizza warm and fresh for as long as it lives.

"So Mort already left?" I ask.

"Yeah," she says. "They wouldn't tell me where he was going or when he's coming back."

"What are you going to do?" I ask.

"They said they'd take me to a safe house on the outskirts of Punk Land," she says.

"I'm supposed to go to the outskirts as well," I say. "Maybe we're going together."

"Maybe," Nan says.

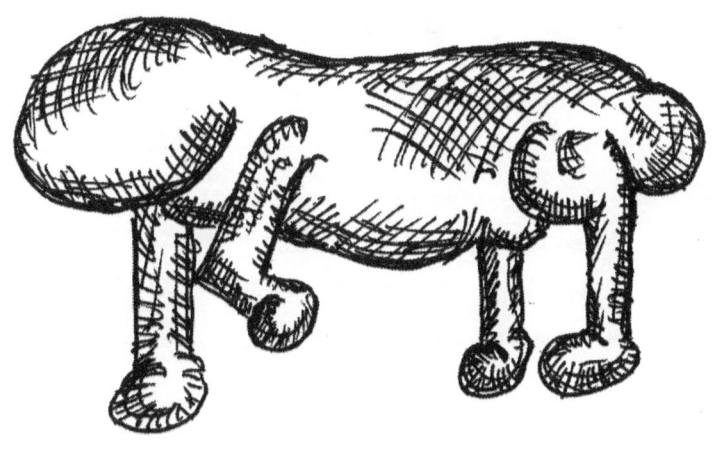

a pizza cat

☺

Nan finds out that Six is taking both of us to the outskirts first thing in the morning. After we get to the safe house, we'll part ways.

It'll be sad. Nan and Mort are the only friends I've got, even though we hardly know each other. Actually, I don't think they ever really liked me at all. I was completely blind to the corruption in Punk Land. I was a follower, an anti-punk. But I'm beginning to learn. I'm beginning to know what it really means to be punk.

The bulletin board above G.G. Allin's office has this message posted:

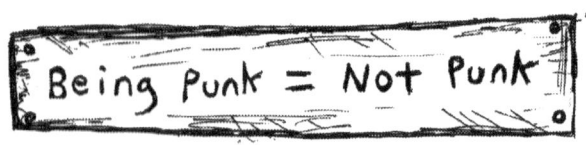

Being Punk = Not Punk

☺

Six yelling at Merle Allin in the turtle room . . .

Six: I'm not a fucking babysitter.

Merle Allin: This is extremely important. You're the only one who can keep him from getting caught.

Six: I'm an assassin. I kill. I don't protect.

Merle Allin: You will be killing more people protecting him than you would in Mosh City.

Six: I want to kill Council members, not Council Police. Anyone can kill Co-

Pos. It takes a shark girl to take out Council members and I'm the only shark girl you've got.

Merle Allin: If you can divert The Council Elite away from our facilities we'll be able to create an army of shark people.

Six: That'll take weeks. I can take out two Council members a day.

Merle Allin: You haven't taken out a single Council member yet.

Six: I haven't been given a chance because you always have me doing bullshit jobs.

Merle Allin: This is not a bullshit job. This is more important than killing Council members. We need a distraction to breed our army.

Six: You have me. You don't need the army.

Merle Allin: You're jealous, that's your problem.

Six: !

Merle Allin: You like being the only shark girl. You're afraid the army will take away your individuality.

Six: I'm the first shark girl. I want to be the first one to attack The Council. And I work alone, not with an army.

Merle Allin: If that's all you're worried about, we can send you in before the others. You can get first crack at The Council.

Six: But in two months?

Merle Allin: Two months isn't long at all. Just hang on for a while. We have to be patient. The only way we can lose now is if we act too soon.

Six: I hate being patient.

☺

A night of halfsleep and scrambled-egg dreams on a plastic couch somewhere deep within the facility, with teenaged pink-haired girls watching Gem cartoons on the floor next to my couch . . .

They giggle a lot and use my floppy parts for a pillow. Their hair itchy against my skin. Almost as bad as sleeping in that bullet belt uniform.

☺

After a morning of centipede soda and hangover zombies walking through the hall-ways, we take one of the mangled SUVs and head out of Scum Fuck. But instead of going south away from civilization, we go west.

"Where are we going?" I say.

Six licks a row of teeth at me.

"The capital," she says.

Nan rests her cheek against the glass.

"But your orders are to take us to the wilderness," I say.

"They weren't orders, they were sug-gestions. We're anarchists."

☺

Driving through lonely roads to the next city . . .

Nan writes in a heavy journal with Breakfast sleeping on a bruised knee. The journal has a title on the cover: The His-tory of the Human Race.

I gaze out of the window at the calm setting. There isn't a sign of civilization for miles.

Punks normally don't wander in the empty spaces between cities. They prefer the urban cityscapes. Since they normally travel between cities in the underground subways, the dirt roads on the surface feel abandoned and dead. We are surrounded by wilderness. Well, not *real* wilderness. It is all someone else's imagination.

In Punk Land, the trees and ground and air seem different from Earth in many ways. My emotional connection with the landscape doesn't feel right.

Perhaps they feel right to Sid Vicious though. This is His version of heaven, so maybe His recreation of nature is just the way he wants it.

Or perhaps this is how he remembers nature. A false memory.

Or perhaps people sense things differently than everyone else. Smells, tastes, colors, and emotional responses are all slightly unique to each being.

Perhaps this landscape doesn't feel right to me because I am experiencing it all through Sid Vicious' senses. These trees are how He saw trees when He was alive. The smells in the air are what He smelled. We are guests in His head, living in His interpretation of the world. It will always feel a little strange and unreal to everyone except Him.

Or perhaps it's something else . . .

☺

We aren't yet going to Mosh City. We're first going to stop off in Pig Slut, the original capital of Punk Land. The main front for the resistance is in the Pig Slut underground, even though Pig Slut is the second most Council-dominant city in all of Punk Land. These rebel forces are our main fist against The Council. They are a well-trained punk army, led by Henry Rollins.

Six says the only reason The Council hasn't overpowered the resistance by now is because of Henry Rollins and his troops. They are an organized fighting machine comparable to Navy SEALs, but with mohawks.

The other leaders and rebels just don't have the discipline of Henry Rollins. Like the guerilla terrorists led by Seth Putnam in the town of Donkey Punch, who pretty much just blow things up without any kind of strategy.

"Rollins is with me on this," Six says to us from the front seat. "He knows that we need to strike now before The Council Elite gets any larger. They're just a po-lice force now. But could become an army at any time."

"He's going to help you get into Mosh City?" I ask. "Even if the Allin brothers are against it?"

"The three leaders rarely agree or work together," Six says. "The agendas of Henry Rollins and G. G. Allin are differ-ent. Rollins will support my idea."

Scene Thirteen
Toilet Tongues

☺

We hide the SUV outside of Pig Slut and head to the city on foot.

"You have to put these on," Six tells us, holding two barcode plates. "Don't let the Co-Pos see you without them."

I take one of the plates. "I thought the barcodes were just tattoos. These are plates."

"The Council has upgraded the tattoos to plastic chips that are surgically implanted into the skin. These are fakes, but the real ones are tracking devices filled with assihol. Whenever somebody's punk points go below the acceptable level, the chip sends an alert to the Co-Po station and then concentrated assihol is injected into the traitor's bloodstream, leaving him unconscious in the street."

She smears an adhesive on my wrist and then presses the chip against the back of my hand. The adhesive is irritating. Worse than getting super glue on your skin. But at least we don't need to have them surgically implanted.

Six continues, "They have complete

control over their people now. Even those who want to go against The Council will not, because of these chips."

"Can't they just remove the chips?" Nan asks.

"Tampering with them, even unintentionally, will automatically drop your punk points to zero, releasing the assihol and alerting the Co-Pos. I've heard stories of co-conspirators helping each other remove their chips, which can be done with ease. The person wearing the chip will be injected with the assihol and go unconscious, but the other will be able to discard the tracking device and take them to a safer side of town. Unfortunately, most conspirators have a hard time finding other conspirators, since everyone is trying to keep up their punk points at all times. And most of the rebels that do remove their chips have a hard time getting out of town. They don't know about Rollins' underground resistance, or any resistance at all. They don't even know there are parts of Punk Land not completely controlled by The Council."

"How are we supposed to blend in?" I ask. "We don't even know what they consider to be proper punk these days."

"Rollins will give us all the information we need. He's surely got up to date copies of the punk guide that his men have studied. They'll know what clothes and attitude we'll have to adapt."

"Do we have to go with you into the capital?" I ask. "Can't we just stay with

Rollins?"

"I'll talk to Rollins about it," Six says. "He might be willing to look after you for me."

☺

We get only a glimpse of the quiet Pig Slut buildings before entering the hidden tunnel that leads to Rollins' underground facility. The city is behind a large stone wall. It looks similar to Victorian-era London, with blue vines crawling up the walls and cool red lights issuing from broken windows.

Beyond Pig Slut, the tips of sky-scrapers from the capital can be seen. A micro Tokyo-esque metropolis stretching high into the grey clouds. You can feel the contrast between the cities, old and new. Dark and light.

☺

Six mentioned the tunnel entrance would be heavily guarded by Rollins' men, but there isn't anyone to be seen.

"They're hiding," Six says. "If they didn't recognize me they would have attacked us by now."

I stare deep into the surrounding trees but can't find any of them. They must have excellent camouflage.

☺

We travel maybe a mile through swampy caverns, filled with a snotty-worm substance and the sound of babies crying from

Sgt. Slaughter!

somewhere distant. There are also stacks of paperback books that are soggy and mulching into the soil. I'm not sure if they were put here by people or if they came from Sid's imagination.

Nan tries to read one of the books but can't find any recognizable words. They must be from Sid's imagination. Or perhaps his subconscious. They are like the unreadable books you find in your dreams.

"Yeah," I hear Six telling Nan, "you'll find odd things in the underground here. Wait until you have to go to the bathroom."

☺

The tunnel opens to an underground neighborhood. With street lights, houses, even lawns. Glowing lights like stars are hanging from the ceiling of the cavern, giving the illusion that we're above ground in a small suburb at night.

"What is this place?" Nan asks.

Shark Girl picks her teeth. "When the resistance was digging an underground headquarters, they stumbled upon this place. A fully functional neighborhood hidden deep below Pig Slut. As if it was waiting for them."

The houses are quiet. There isn't any movement in the streets. Windows are wide open to clean, brightly lit living rooms. Like display homes. The first dozen houses, empty and sterile.

"Where is everyone?" Nan asks.

"Probably in the mansion," Six says.

☺

At the end of the block, the road ends at a large white house with plastic rose bushes. The smell of wet paint fills my nostrils as we knock on the door.

No answer.

Knock again.

"Nobody's home," I say.

Six flicks her lips.

"They must be on a mission," she says.

Nan peeks through a window. "I see someone in there."

"What's he doing?" I ask.

"Just sitting there," Nan says. "Wait. There's some other people in the kitchen. Just standing there."

Six opens the front door.

It is like a wax museum inside. The people are not people, they are figures standing in odd poses. All of them dis-played in a party scene. Punks in drinking and fighting positions.

"What are these things?" Nan asks.

Six is busy examining the figures. "These aren't Rollins' men."

She enters the kitchen, checks out all of the figures. "Where the hell is he?"

Unlike the insides of the other houses, this place is trashed. I have to balance myself to keep from tripping over broken furniture, rotten food, and beer bottles.

☺

The figures aren't fake. They are real people.

"They're all on cyclost," Six says.

"A hallucinogenic drug. As a side effect, it freezes you in time for about half an hour once you start to come down."

"They're frozen?" Nan asks, waving her hand in front of a fat zit-bearded skinhead.

"Idiots," Six says. "The Co-Pos could come in here and take them all down and they wouldn't even realize it."

We wander the mansion, finding frozen people in every room.

"Did every single one of them take it?" Nan asks. "You'd think at least one of them would have decided to pass."

"Not if these punks are who I think they are," Six says.

"Who do you think they are?" Nan asks.

☺

"Anal Cunt," Six says as she opens the door to the master bedroom.

Frozen in rocking chairs sits the band Anal Cunt. Their singer and leader of the guerilla rebel army, Seth Putnam, is in the middle of drinking a shot of assihol. The drink, however, did not freeze in time and some of it has spilled into his lap.

"Seth, you asshole," Shark Girl says.

She pushes one of his friends out of his chair who falls over frozen, still in the seated position. Then pulls herself up close to Seth's face, so that she'll be the first thing he sees once he returns to the present.

☺

An hour passes, he's still frozen.

Six has grown tired of sitting an inch away from the man's face and is now rocking in her chair, trying to be patient.

Nan is lying on the urine-scented bed, falling asleep.

"Are they going to be frozen forever?" I ask.

The shark girl kicks a shot glass of assihol across the room.

☺

It's another twenty minutes or so before Seth Putnam fades back into liveliness. The first movement out of him are globs of sweat dripping out of his moppy hair.

His friends stay frozen.

Eyes crooked at Six and his lips curling up, Seth opens his mouth to speak but instead of words he coughs out assihol and piles out of his chair.

"Where the fuck is Rollins, Seth?" Six asks, pushing him so that he doesn't fall on her.

Seth shakes his head, goes to the dresser and pulls a new bottle of assihol out of his underwear.

His response is, "Fuck . . ."

"What's going on?" she asks, tightening fists.

He's still out of it, spitting slobber words out of his mouth.

"What are your people doing in Pig Slut?"

He shakes his head and stumbles out of the room.

"Stupid cunt," he says from the hallway.

☺

Seth disappears into the mansion. We go through the hallways looking for him. The party has been brought back from its sleep. People are animated again, drinking and punching. Some people are still frozen and get dicks drawn on their necks and chins, pointing up at their mouths.

Six is calm, which probably means she's really pissed off. Any punk that gets in her way she knocks on his ass.

We find Seth again downstairs with his friend, Josh, looking through Rollins' music collection. Everything he picks up he calls "gay" and tosses it over his shoulder.

"Where's Rollins?" Six asks him again.

But Seth is busy saying, "Gay . . . Gay . . . Gay . . ."

"I'm going to kill him," she whispers to me.

"Fuck it," Seth says, after tossing the last cassette. "Music sucks anyway."

He takes a drink of assihol and shakes his head at Six.

"What the fuck are *you* doing here?" Seth asks.

"We're trying to get into the capital," she says. "What happened to Rollins?"

"He was fucking captured days ago," he says. "Tick-Tock set a trap for him, and the dumbass fag fell for it. So we moved in and took over."

"What have you accomplished since you took command?" she asks.

He shrugs.

"This is the front line," she says. "You're in place to do the most damage. The revolution depends on this."

Seth just impersonates the shark girl in a whiney voice, "Uhhn, I'm Six and I care about the revolution," and walks away.

☺

Six charges after Seth to continue the conversation, but I don't follow her. I have to go to the bathroom.

Upstairs, I find an odd closet that is supposed to be a bathroom. Inside, there is a toilet made out of meat and fingers.

This place is definitely part of Sid Vicious' subconscious mind.

While shitting, the toilet hole breathes against my ass. Sometimes it gurgles or burps as my logs drop into its mouth.

Wet tongues gush into my ass as I shit, licking the area clean.

Sitting here with toilet tongues penetrating me, I think of the good old times.

I miss Frog Strips.

I miss Tekky too.

☺

When I get back to the party, all of the punks are crowded in the living room, getting ready to take more cyclost. Six

20 THINGS SETH PUTNAM THINKS ARE GAY

Allston
softball
technology
recycling
art school
music
having goals
tribal tattoos
windchimes
this book
Harvey Korman
the word 'anarchy'
the members of Drop Dead
people who don't like The Village People
anyone who cares about anything
the word 'homophobic'
Kim Goss's tattoo
Chris Barnes
all of his fans
you

and Nan are standing behind Seth; Nan is laughing with him for some reason.

"Uhhn, I'm Goblin and I'm in love with a dildo," Seth says to me as I come down the stairs.

His friends all look at me and laugh. Six must have told him all about me. I hide behind Nan as soon as I arrive and watch them take their drugs.

The cylost is a clear film that they put into their eyes like contact lenses. It dissolves in their tears and is absorbed directly into their sight.

"Want some?" Seth asks me, holding some cyclost lenses.

I accept them. I don't know why.

"Don't do it," Six says to me. "This stuff is too strong for you. The side-effects are unpredictable."

Nan doesn't take it either. Since she's alive, it would probably kill her.

☺

I get separated from the girls, wandering through the dazed punks on their cyclost trips.

"Need help with those?" Josh asks, pointing at the cyclost lenses still in my hands.

Before I can get away, the Anal Cunt guitarist helps me put the drugs into my eyes. He's actually very nice, but I don't know how to tell him I'd prefer to stay sober.

"There ya go," he says, cleaning his glasses.

In just a few minutes, things begin to sparkle and fizz inside of my brain. Inky visuals begin pooling in the corners of my eyes.

Behind me, I can hear Seth garble-laughing with his friends, saying stuff like "Uhhn, I'm Greg and I like it when the tongues lick my asshole" or calling things gay.

My legs get weak, so I look for an unbroken couch. The only one not in use by frozen people is up in Rollins' office. It is empty and quiet. I feel the drug beginning to peak. Light gleaming from the metal of Rollins' desk becomes angelic. The texture of my fingers becomes like hard canvas.

My eyes roll into the back of my head like shark girl taking a bite of a sandwich . . .

Scene Fourteen
Scorpion Bubbles

☺

I click back into time.

Must have been frozen.

It doesn't feel like I was frozen. It's not like falling asleep and waking up. The only reason I feel like I had been frozen in time is because I am no longer on the couch in Rollins' office.

I am sitting on a hard white bed in a very clean room with light grey walls and dark grey carpeting. I am all alone and mostly nude. Somebody has removed my bullet belt encasing.

Looking down: there is writing all over my skin.

I go to a mirror: While out of it, I have been tagged with crude penis drawings and insults to my sexuality.

Also, there are these words on my back:

Uhhn. I'm Goblin and I've been frozen in time for ten days.

Ten days? Is that a joke?

Perhaps I had an allergic reaction to the cyclost and have been stuck in time for longer than usual.

I open the blinds and take a look out of the window: a city.

This isn't one of the empty houses in the underground. It is an apartment. I'm in the capital.

I'm in Mosh City.

☺

The buildings are colorless and higher than my eyes can see. There aren't people anywhere. Not walking on the sidewalk below, not in the apartments across the street. It is a ghost metropolis.

The apartment is quiet. I call out. Nan, Six, Seth Putnam. Nobody is here with me. There's a pile of clothes and bullet belts in the living room, but it is the only sign that this apartment has actually been lived in.

A smacking noise, from a neighboring apartment . . . Somebody slapping against the walls. This isn't a ghost metropolis. People are just very quiet here. Hidden. Was I being too loud?

Another slap.

I'm not being loud at all now. Perhaps my footsteps caused a rumbling in the floor. I stop moving.

Slap. Slap. Slap.

Am I breathing too loud?

Slap-slap.

Wait a minute . . .

Slap.

That sound isn't coming from outside of the apartment . . .

Slap, slap, slap.

It's in . . .

Slap, slap.

The bathroom.

☺

Inside the bathroom:

A clean white room with soft grey lighting. Sterile white shower curtain. A hospital's bathroom.

The noise must have come from the other side of the wall.

SLAP.

A sliding noise against porcelain.

Wait . . .

There's something inside of the bathtub.

I rip open the shower curtain to reveal a pile of meat and gore in the tub.

Corpses.

There are three skeletons folded together. Most of their meat missing from their bones. Limbs amputated. Black blood smeared across the white walls.

And they are still alive. The top skeleton, sitting mostly upright, rolls its eyeballs within its skull at me. It tries to move its arms but they lack muscle. Still, I see the bits of shredded muscle flexing on the bone, trying desperately to move.

Only one corpse leg has strength enough to slap its foot-peelings against the bathroom wall.

I turn off the light and close the door, back away from the slapping noises as the front door opens behind me.

☺

It's Nan.

She wears a white jumpsuit and has a small white mohawk.

"You're back," she says in a soft voice, carefully squeezing the door shut behind her.

"I—"

She hushes me before I can speak.

Waves me to follow her into the bedroom closet. We crowd together in the dark.

"Got to be quiet," she says.

"What's going on?" I whisper.

"You've been out of it for a long time," Nan says. "But we were hoping you'd be frozen for longer."

"I didn't want to come here," I say. "I told Six I wanted to stay in Pig Slut."

"She didn't want to leave you with Seth Putnam," Nan says. "You're safer with her."

"Where is she?"

"She's hunting The Council Elite. Trying to find their headquarters. You'll need to study the punk rulebook. It's going to be difficult for you because of the way you look. Make sure you know as many rules as possible. The Co-Pos pay close attention to the deformed ones."

"Why?"

"You don't fit in," she says. "They're

looking for any excuse to put all the deformed punks away. Very few of them are left. Break the tiniest rule and you're screwed."

"Don't worry," I say. "I'm not leaving this apartment."

"Unfortunately," Nan says, "that's not possible. You need to eat. Unless you want to starve to death over and over again, you'll have to leave the apartment."

"Can't you just bring food back to me?" I ask.

"That's not the way it works here. If you're hungry, you have to leave the apartment. You'll see what I mean. Just read the rulebook."

"I might prefer starving to death over and over again . . ." I say.

☺

"Oh wait . . ." I whisper to Nan as she leaves the closet. "Who are the dead people in the bathroom?"

She smiles. "They are shark girl's friends."

☺

Nan drops a heavy box on my lap. No, not a box. A book.

The cover reads:

The Official Punk Rulebook.

It is this big:

It has to be 50,000 pages long!

It'll take months to memorize all of this! If it's even possible!

"Just skim through it," Nan says. "I don't think anybody has it all memorized. Not even the Co-Pos."

I open the book. The text is very small. There is so much information packed in that it makes me dizzy trying to read it.

"I've just been following what everyone else does," Nan says. "You'll pick up the basics pretty quick."

"Basics?" I ask.

"You'll see. We'll go when you're ready."

I don't think I'll ever be ready.

☺

I put on a white jumpsuit and a white skipper hat. These are the only clothes that are considered punk. The only punk hairstyle is a short white mohawk. If you don't have a short white mohawk you must wear the hat.

We take a small metal elevator down to street level. The slight humming noise in the elevator is the only sound for miles. Once it stops, all we can hear is the mist rising off puddles in the street. There isn't color here. Everything seems to be the same shade of bright grey.

"Follow my lead," Nan says. Her voice barely a whisper but it still echoes through the empty streets.

☺

What I got from the rulebook was much different from any previous Idiot's Guide to Being Punk. This one isn't just about style and attitude, it's about how you must live your life from second to second.

We can't just walk down the street the way we want to. There are footprints painted bright-bright grey on the sidewalk that we must step on, one set of prints per direction. Our feet must be placed just perfectly on the prints. Two inches apart, with the range of each step being two feet, regardless of the length of your legs. Our walking speed has to be 20 steps a minute, so we must count to three between each step. This is all a difficult process because our eyes must be at a 75 degree angle

at all time. We're not allowed to look at
our feet. Luckily, I have Nan ahead of me
and can mimic her movements.

"You'll get the rhythm of it soon,"
Nan says. "It's best to practice when nobody is around."

Tripping or falling out of rhythm is
not considered punk and you'll lose punk
points if you do this while a Co-Po is
around.

Besides the counting of three between
each step, we must also count the footsteps. Every eighth footstep, we must put
our hands on our hips and hold them there
for eight more footsteps, then they can go
back to swinging at our sides. While not on
your hips, your arms must swing with each
step.

Every once in a while there will be
footprints with symbols painted on them.
When stepping on a symbol, you must do
something depending on the symbol.

This symbol is the only one we will
come across today:

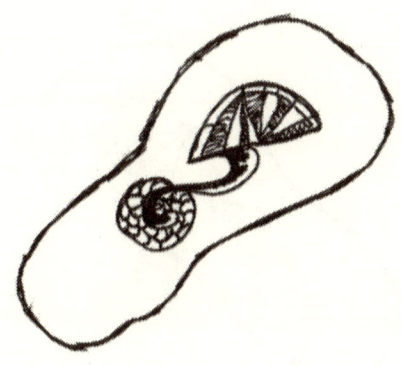

When I step on it, I'll have to poke my chin with my thumb twice and then pull on my ear.

Nan says the rulebook has pages and pages filled with maps of all the foot-prints in the city, explaining where every symboled print is located and what you are supposed to do when you step on them.

When stepping on this footprint, you must point up and then point down:

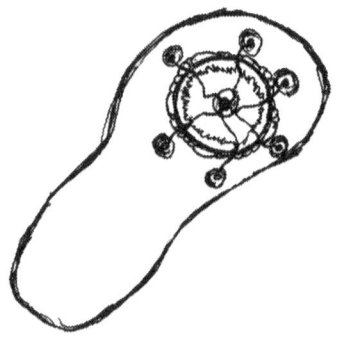

On this footprint, you must flare your nostrils:

Some symbols are luxury symbols. Like this:

You are allowed to scratch your nose if you step on that symbol.

Or this:

You can stop for ten seconds and stretch your legs, as long as nobody is behind you.

Some of these symboled prints are very complex.

Like this one:

If you are to step on that, you have to do something different depending on the hour of the month. Which means, there are 720 different actions you must memorize for that step alone. Sometimes you have to pull on an ear. Sometimes you have to say the alphabet in three seconds before you go to the next step. It is near impossible, and there are over a dozen equally compli- cated symbols on the footprint map. Nan thinks everybody loses punk points on some symbols. It isn't possible to memorize them all.

☺

There doesn't seem to be a way to gain punk points anymore. Back when I was an authority on punk, the point system was a way to reward those who were punk and pun- ish those who were not. Now people just have to try to hold on to the punk points they have for as long as they can.

☺

I blink ten times fast. The rulebook
says it isn't punk to blink at random, so
you have to hold your eyes open wide for
ten seconds and then blink 10 times.

The rulebook says in large black letters on the back:

Perfection = Punk

☺

Nan said I would get used to the rhythm
by now, but I still have to glance down at
my feet to see where my feet are landing.
I'm far too deformed to walk properly.
Now there are people up ahead and I'm
walking even sloppier. It's hard to concentrate with others nearby. They aren't
Co-Pos, but still make me nervous. One of
them is tapping his cheek as he walks. I
have no idea why. Perhaps you have to tap
your cheek all day if you sleep in a minute
too long.

☺

There are not many places to stop and
rest in this city. It is designed so that
nobody lingers. Nobody has a chance to be
lazy. Even while eating.
We enter a tunnel lined with hoses
that spray bubbles at us. Ahead, the entire tunnel is so packed with these bubbles
that you can hardly see where you're going. The bubbles make squishy-fart noises
as they rub against each other in the air.

It smells beefy and rotten in here.

"What's going on?" I ask Nan, not able to whisper over the bubbling noises.

"Breathe in the bubbles," she says.

"Why?"

"That's how they eat here. They are filled with all the nutrients you need to survive."

I inhale some of the bubbles and cough as they pop in my throat. Gasoline fumes rise out of my mouth.

"They're horrible!" I say.

She says, "They are called scorpion bubbles. Made from the juices of insects. It's the only food they have in the city so you'll have to get used to them."

I suck some more into my mouth and swallow; a buttery grey slime coats my throat and gags me until I spew it out.

The tangy lard flavor is too intense. I don't eat anymore, breathing through my nostrils, occasionally licking the pungent fluid from bubbles that pop on my lips. It's almost better to starve myself to death over and over again than go through this walking and eating process everyday. I'm not surprised there aren't many people out on the streets.

Unless the majority of the people have already been kicked out of Punk Land for losing all their punk points . . .

☺

Once we exit the feeding tunnel, we see a mini-SUV parked on the side of the road. Two Co-Pos are pushing around an obese teenaged girl, laughing at her as she attempts to balance on the sidewalk and touch her elbows to her knees.

We're going to have to walk right by them. There is a procedure you can do to turn around and change directions, but Nan doesn't know it yet. She can just turn corners. And there isn't a corner to turn before we reach the police.

One of the officers sees us approaching. He smiles through his bright red mustache at Nan. She's probably doing something wrong. Maybe we are supposed to be tapping our cheeks today.

The red-mustache cop leaves the obese young girl's elbow-knee-tapping to his partner, and steps toward us. He doesn't use the footprints. His steps and blinks are without pattern.

☺

Once Nan hits her eighth step and her hands go to her hips, she wiggles her thumb at me behind her waist as if it's some kind of signal.

She stops in her tracks and knocks on her stomach at the man. Then turns to her left and steps in front of the door of the building next to us. She draws an invisible circle on the door with her finger, then pokes the center of the circle, and enters the building.

I imitate her, but do it very quickly, hoping the cop doesn't notice I am deformed.

☺

We don't look back, stepping quickly
through the hallway of the apartment building toward the other side.

The door opens behind me. I can feel
the chubby man smiling at us, twisting his
mustache. Nan's pace slows down slightly.
Back to the standard rhythm. I don't hear
the apartment door close, or the man's
feet stepping after us. He's probably just
standing there in the doorway, watching.

We've missed the stairwell, so he must
know we don't live here. He can see we are
just cutting through the building so we
can avoid him.

When Nan gets to the other door, she
doesn't do the circle with her finger. She
just opens it and darts around the corner
as quick as she can.

Then fast-walks down the sidewalk back
to home base.

☺

"You didn't do the circle-thing," I
tell her as she fast-walks.

"That circle-thing isn't in the
rulebook," she says. "I made it up, hoping
the cop would be too confused to stop us.
I doubt they know all the rules."

Before we get back to the apartment,
we hear a mini-SUV creep-driving up the
street behind us. I slow to regulation
speed, but Nan moves faster.

"Shouldn't we act natural?" I ask.

"They can't see how fast we're walking yet," she says. "If we can get inside

the apartment building, we'll be safe."

I speed up, skipping the footprints but still putting my hands on and off my hips as I go. The automobile catches up. I try getting back onto the footprints, but Nan is moving even faster now. The Co-Pos pull over ahead of us, parking on the side-walk to block our path. Right in front of the elevator.

They don't get out. Just cutting off our route and waiting for us to react.

The elevator is still at ground-level. If we were just a minute sooner we could have made it.

"Let's go!" Nan says.

She lunges forward at the elevator, squeezing between the SUV and the build-ing. I follow, but I am so deformed and awkward compared to her. It isn't as easy for me to squeeze through.

"Come on," she cries.

She's inside now. The Co-Pos step out of the SUV. They don't say a word. A black-bearded cop looks at me from one side of the SUV and the red-mustached cop is smil-ing at me from the other.

I push myself harder until I fall into the elevator carpet.

Nan closes the door and hits buttons for several floors.

"What are you doing?" I ask.

"We don't want them to know where we're getting off," she says.

"They're going to tear this whole building apart looking for us!"

"Not necessarily," she says. "We

haven't really done anything wrong besides missing a few steps to avoid confrontation. It probably happens all the time."

"But they're already suspicious of us," I say. "We'll never be able to leave the building again."

"They aren't very persistent," she says. "They'll forget about us soon enough."

The elevator door opens and closes on a zombie-like woman with a patchy crooked white mohawk. She doesn't even look at us. Just stands there.

"Of course," Nan says, "the Co-Pos really do hate deformed people . . ."

☺

We dart out of the elevator when it gets to our level and leap into our apartment.

Before we close the door, I see a figure entering from the stairwell.

"Crap," I say as Nan locks the door. "Somebody's out there."

"Co-Po?" she asks.

I shrug.

Turning around, we see a naked woman gagged and hog-tied on the living room floor. She doesn't have the regulation short white mohawk. Instead, she has three tall silver spikes lined horizontally from ear to ear, a Statue of Liberty look.

"It's Ariel," Nan says.

"Who?" I ask.

"One of The Council Heads," she says.

There are four knocks at the door.

We freeze.

The woman tries to scream through her gag.

"Council Police," says the man behind the door.

Damn Six and damn Nan for getting me into this!

There are four more knocks.

"Help me get her out of here," Nan says.

We grab the woman by her feet and shoulders, try to lift her. But Nan is too small and I am too deformed to get her off the ground. I start dragging her across the carpet, but only get a couple inches before the door unlocks from the other side and swings open.

The red-mustached cop stands in the doorway.

His smile falls from his face as he sees us standing over one of the highest ranking members of the Punk Council.

Scene Fifteen
Disease Bikini

☺

We don't move until the cop pulls his gun and starts shooting assihol bullets at us.

Nan ducks behind the naked woman and I use a pile of bullet belts as a shield.

"Henry!" cries the cop to the stairwell.

Six enters from the bathroom. Topless. Blood dripping from her mouth and smeared across her breasts. She's like some kind of crazed demon with an enormous blue mohawk.

The red-mustached man staggers back, points his gun at her.

"Get back!"

She smiles at him. The same smile he was giving to me.

Her eyes roll in and out of her head as she bends her neck at him.

The cop steps up to her and points the barrel at her face. "I said—"

She cuts him off by twisting the gun out of his hand and firing it into his throat. The assihol bullet doesn't break inside of him. It pierces through the soft neck skin and hits the wall behind him.

The cop's neck dribbles with blood and when he calls out for his partner only blood splats out of his voice box. Six smiles wide as she leans into him, opens her mouth to reveal rows of teeth and bites deep into the man's throat.

She fires the gun three times in his belly as she chews his throat open.

The bondaged woman on the floor is screaming so loud that the gag is not enough to silence her.

Nan has to kick her in the head until she blanks out.

☺

Bullets fly into the room at Six, hitting the walls and the chubby back of the throatless cop in Six's arms. She drops Red Mustache and approaches Black Beard in the stairwell. Her breasts are now so bloody you can hardly tell she is topless.

Shark Girl fires five shots at Black Beard. He tumbles back and turns to run. All of her bullets miss. She isn't trying to hit him, just scare him a little. Get him moving.

"She loves chasing her prey," Nan says.

Black Beard races down the stairs and Six follows casually after, pulling her underwear out of the crack of her ass.

☺

She returns with his body a few minutes later. His legs chewed off at the knees. Two bullet holes in the center of his skull.

"What the hell happened?" Six asks Nan, throwing one of Black Beard's legs at her.

"They followed us!" Nan says.

"You led them right to our location," Six says. "We have enough Council flesh to worry about without bringing any Co-Pos in here."

"I'm sorry," Nan says. "Goblin needed to learn how to get the scorpion bubbles."

"I didn't want him leaving to eat scorpion bubbles," Six says. "I wanted him to stay here and help me dispose of the Council members."

"You didn't tell me that," Nan says. "You said you hoped he stayed frozen until we left the capital."

"Well, we need him here. Especially now."

"Sorry," Nan says.

Six uses one of the white couch cushions to wipe the blood from her breasts. Then strips the red-mustached cop of his clothes.

"I'm going to go ditch their SUV on the other side of town," Six says as she pulls on the Co-Po uniform. "I'll be back in an hour. Clean the blood out of the stairway while I'm gone."

"And here . . ." she gives me a pistol and a handful of assihol bullets. "Shoot them again if they regain consciousness."

On her way out the door, she turns back and says to me, "Welcome back," while licking blood from the corner of her mouth.

☺

An hour later and Six hasn't returned.
Another hour passes.
Nan shoots each of the cops in the chest before they get a chance to wake up.
"I don't like this," Nan says. "She's never late."
Another hour passes.
"If she doesn't come back in a few hours we'll have to leave," Nan says.
"Where will we go?" I ask.
"Back to Seth Putnam's camp, I guess. See if we can get transportation back to Scum Fuck."
"We shouldn't be in the capital anyway."

☺

A few more hours pass.
The cops are coming back to consciousness but Nan doesn't want to waste anymore bullets on them. We might need them on our way out of town.
We tie up the cops with sheets and bullet belts.
"It's not going to be enough," Nan says.
The Council woman has stopped struggling, stopped trying to scream. She just lies on the floor next to the couch, slowly blinking her eyes at me.

☺

We should have left by now, but neither of us can get ourselves to go.
The black-bearded cop opens his eyes

a sticker on the bathroom mirror:

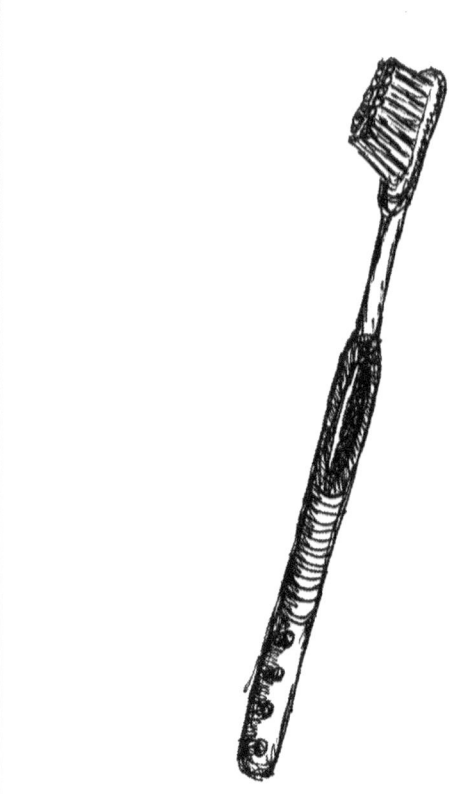

**BRUSHING YOUR TEETH 150 TIMES
VERTICALLY AND 150 TIMES HORIZONTALLY
EVERY 150 MINUTES = PUNK**

and groans at us. His brain spins behind his face. He pukes onto his chest and gasps for air.

"Don't bother screaming," Nan says.

"Huh?" he squints his eyes at Nan as his tongue rolls inside of his mouth.

Blood dribbles down his face from the holes in his head.

She has her gun pointed at him. "If you scream again I'll have to pump more of that poison into you."

"Ehn," he says.

"Nobody in this apartment building cares, anyway," she says. "You were screaming all through this place and not a single tenant reported it."

"What's going on?" he says.

"You're dead," Nan says.

"Huh?" he says.

He straightens his face and his eyes calm.

"My legs . . ." he cries.

Now he remembers.

"What was that bitch?" he asks.

"A friend of ours," Nan says.

"She bit my legs off!" he cries.

"Yeah, she tends to do that," Nan says.

"She chewed right through them like they were celery!"

"She didn't want you to get away."

"Untie me," he says. "Quick! Before she gets back!"

Nan says, "No."

He looks surprised at her answer. "Do you know who I am?"

"Nobody important," Nan says.

"I am Council Police! You must show me respect!"

"Not anymore," she says. "You're dead now."

"Council Police can't die. Only civilians have to follow the rules."

"We disagree," Nan says.

"You can't disagree!"

"We've taken you out. You, your partner, Ariel over there. All of you are going to play fair for a change and stay dead. Six will make sure of that."

"Ariel?" the cop finally notices the naked woman on the couch. "You've got Ariel?"

The naked woman's eyes tear up again.

"Oh, you people," the cop chuckles at us, "you don't know how much shit you're in. They're going to shut this whole town down once they find out Ariel is missing. A task force is going to come in here and take you out by the end of the day."

"They haven't come yet," Nan says. "And the day is almost over."

"Just wait and see," he says. "Tick-Tock's men never fail."

"They failed to stop Six from breaking us out of prison," Nan says. "She took care of them quicker than she did you."

"Bullshit," he says. "You're all so fucked!"

He laughs at us.

"You won't be laughing once Shark Girl gets back."

He continues laughing.

☺

Shark Girl walks in on the conversation, as if on cue.

The cop isn't laughing anymore. He stares at his legs like they are somebody else's.

"What took you so long?" Nan asks.

"Co-Pos everywhere," she says, taking off the police uniform.

"We thought you were captured," Nan says. "We were going to leave."

"You wouldn't have gotten far," she says, looking through a pile of clothes for a top.

"I told you!" Black Beard says. "Tick-Tock will tear this city apart looking for Ariel!"

Six drops the clothes and turns to the policeman, walks over to him topless. It's as if she enjoys exposing her breasts to the people she kills.

"Tick-Tock can come and try," she says.

"You don't have a chance," he says. A little more timid than he was with Nan. "He'll be coming here anytime now. And I'll be laughing my ass off at you."

"Oh, but you won't," Six says, sitting on the man's stumps. "You see, you're dead now. You're going to the dead people's home."

"We don't use the dead people's home anymore," he says.

"I know," Six pouts at him. "But we still have to take you out of the game."

"How do you plan to do that?" he asks. "You can't possibly keep me sedated forever."

"I don't plan on sedating you," she says, forcing her breasts into his face. "I'm going to eat you."

She opens her mouth to expose rows of teeth, drool slipping over her lips.

"I can chew through bone," she says. "There's no part of you that I can't digest."

Teasing him, acting as if the thought turns her on, she grinds her crotch hard into his lap and presses her stomach against his cheek.

"Eventually, you'll regenerate from my shit," she says, "but you'll be trapped miles underground, where nobody will ever find you."

She smiles at him. Their eyes locked on one another.

He shakes his head *no* at her and she nods her head *yes*, then licks the blood from the bullet holes in his face.

"What do you think happened to the Council members who disappeared last week?" she asks.

Now he believes she's serious.

☺

He opens his mouth to scream, but she covers it with her hand and bites into the back of his neck. He muffle-cries for our help, tears running from his eyes, begging Six to stop. But she continues to rip the flesh from his body with her shark-like teeth, swallowing him chunk by chunk.

She rubs his blood on her breasts and

licks her lips at him. I think she's getting ready to fuck him.

Shark girls must be eating and fucking machines.

"Let's go," Nan says. "This will get really ugly."

We stand up to go. The silver-spiked Council woman is screaming behind her gag again. From her angle, she can't see what is happening. She can only see a tall blue mohawk peeking out from behind the couch like a shark fin, thrashing around to tear pieces of meat off of the victim.

And she knows the same thing will soon happen to her.

☺

I wake up next to Nan several hours later.

Breakfast is crawling on my chest, pushing at me, as if I'm lying too close to Nan and he's getting jealous. I pick up the living hand and place him on the other side of Nan. The hand wiggles its fingers at me.

"Where the heck have you been?" I ask the hand.

Breakfast leaps off the bed and scurries across the floor like a spider.

☺

I go into the living room.

The black-bearded cop isn't moving anymore. The upper half of his body is missing. His shoulders, arms, and head have been chewed off. Pieces of skull and fingers are scattered across the floor, but

I'm sure most of what's missing is in Six's gut right now.

The Council woman is sitting on the couch. She isn't bound or gagged anymore. Just sitting there, staring at me. Both of her arms have been taken off.

"Goblin," Six calls to me from the other room. "Here. I need help with this."

She enters carrying one of the woman's arms.

Six hands the arm to me and plops onto the couch. "Finish this one for me. I can't eat another bite."

I look at the partially eaten limb. The woman it used to belong to is watching me.

"I can't eat this," I say.

"You have to," Six says, groaning at her full belly. "We've got a lot of people to get rid of."

"Can't we just chop them up and flush them down the toilet?" I ask.

"I tried that once and the toilet got backed up," she says. "Besides, we need to eat and can't risk going out to get scorpion bubbles every day."

"Nan goes out," I say.

"She can blend in better than we can."

I like the idea of staying off the streets, but eating human flesh?

"Just think of it as rare beef," Six says.

It is for a good cause. I might be able to eat people if it benefits the rebellion . . .

I open my mouth around the arm.

"I can't," I say. "She's looking at me."

"So," Six says.

"I don't want her to see me eat her arm," I say.

"Just do it," Six says. "I think she's catatonic anyway. She hasn't moved or said a word since I bit her limbs off."

I see her watching me as I bite into her arm again. The hand clenches a fist at me and I drop it on the floor.

"It's alive!" I say.

"Yeah," she says. "Body parts tend to move on their own for some reason. Just wait until after you eat them and they start squirming inside of you. It's quite an experience."

I pick up the limb and try again, quickly so that it doesn't move. I bite but nothing happens. Try again. I can't tear any meat off.

"My mouth doesn't work right," I say.

"Here, I'll help you," Six says.

She takes the arm from me and bites into it with her shark teeth. Spits out a chunk and hands it to me. I take the piece and put it in my mouth. It's rubbery and perfume-scented. The woman watches me as I swallow a piece of her.

Six chews the arm up into several tiny pieces for me.

"Let me know if you can't swallow the bones. We'll have to grind them into powder if they become a problem."

I eat the pieces, pretending they are regular food and aren't human at all. The fingers make it difficult to pretend. I might have to skip the fingers.

☺

A few hours pass.

Six is ready to eat again.

She goes to the woman and examines her body, thinking about what part of her she'd like to eat. Using her sense of smell, she explores the woman's skin. Once she reaches the breasts, Six backs up.

"What is it?" I ask.

The shark girl sniffs at the woman's breasts again. "She's wearing a disease bikini."

"A what?" I ask.

"It's a common weapon used among female assassins. The bikini is a gelatin film dried to the breasts. It contains a deadly virus that is released during oral contact. It's particularly nasty here in Punk Land, because those infected with the virus will be killed over and over again. The virus continues to spread through the host and the body will never be able to heal itself completely. The virus will continue to destroy the flesh as soon as it regenerates. You'll be a rotten immobilized corpse for all eternity."

"Was any on her arm?" I ask. "Am I infected?"

"No," Six says. "I would have smelled it."

"Why is she wearing it anyway?" I ask.

"She's not an assassin," Six says. "Not on our side, anyway. I didn't know they had assassins on their side."

"I'm not on their side," the armless woman says, wide awake and staring at us.

☺

"I was going to infect Johnny Rotten," the woman says. "Before you captured me."

Her voice is calm. She doesn't seem too alarmed that her limbs have been eaten.

"Not all of us are bad people," she says. "Most of us just wanted some order. We were sick of anarchy. Punk was fun for a while, but it got old. We didn't want to live in chaos forever."

"So you turned it into this?" Six asks.

"We don't know how things got out of control. Johnny Rotten is insane. We have to overthrow him before it gets worse."

"I thought Rotten wasn't running the show," Six says. "He's just a puppet."

"No," she says. "It's all him. You have to let me go so I can seduce him and infect him as planned. This virus would incapacitate him long enough for us to take over."

Six laughs at her. "I doubt you can seduce anyone without arms."

"Once they grow back, then," she says.

"I'll consider it," Six peels the disease bikini from the woman's breasts. "But I think it might be best to just get rid of you."

Even if she's telling the truth . . .

Scene Sixteen
Stomach Ghosts

☺

Weeks go by.

Six has eaten both of the cops and the skeletons in the bathroom. Disposing their bodies down the sewer pipes to the baby underground.

Every day she will go out, hunt down a member of the punk elite. She doesn't follow any of the rules of the citizens. Doesn't wear the proper clothes or step on the right footprints, but she's too fast for anyone to notice, too quiet.

She swims under the wind and through shadows at her victim, firing just a single bullet and carrying the body back into the shadows.

They have no reason to suspect there is an assassin taking them out. They believe these missing members of the elite are betrayers of The Council who have joined forces with the rebellion. Not only are they losing their numbers, but they believe their enemy is gaining in number.

She'll always return with somebody, pumped full of assihol. We'll cut apart the body and eat as much as we can. Six can eat almost half of a human a day. We usually finish them off. I tend to puke them up a lot, which is usually good because it can be flushed down the toilet and I'll have room to eat more.

But I am dying to leave this city.

It seems Six isn't willing to leave unless we're caught or have finally eaten everyone.

☺

Ariel is still around. My job is to keep an eye on her at all times. Shoot her if necessary. Nan carries a gun as well, just in case I can't handle her.

Six doesn't believe her story about using the disease bikini on Johnny Rotten. Everyone can tell he is just an empty shell. If she would have said Tick-Tock we would have believed her. Or anyone with power besides Rotten. Of course, she could be ignorant to the fact that Rotten has nothing to do with the state of Punk Land. The citizens that have been loyal to The Council are usually pretty gullible.

So Six is keeping her around for now. She's not one of us. Just a prisoner. And she eats people with us, which has definitely been a help. Though it is a bit grotesque to see her eating human flesh with her baby arms that have not fully grown back yet. She's like a tyrannosaurus rex.

☺

Shark Girl really does fuck what she

Photos of Shark Girl in Mosh City

eats. She doesn't just tease her victims before eating them. She molests them.

I've started watching her.

I don't think she minds that I watch or maybe she doesn't realize I am there. She kind of goes into her own little world with her prey.

She likes to tell her prisoners what she is going to do to them, explains how she will chew and digest their meat. She'll strip them naked and explore their flesh, smelling them, licking the salt from their skin. If they aren't very clean, she might take them into the shower.

Then she fucks them . . . and eats them while fucking them.

"It's the best orgasm they'll ever have," Six tells me.

☺

I think Tekky would have gotten along with Six.

At least while eating people. Like the shark girl, I'm sure she would find it sexually arousing to molest and eat someone.

Tekky used to make little men out of hot dogs and eat them. She'd usually cut arms and legs in the meat. Poke holes for the eyes and mouth. The pants would be chili or sauerkraut. Cheese for a shirt. Mustard for a tie and hair. Sometimes ketchup for buttons. She'd make a few different variations of hot dog people and play on the coffee table with them before she'd bite pieces off and make crying noises for them. It seems cute and playful, but Tekky had a way of turning the cute and playful into something disturbingly sexual. Perhaps it was the way she glared at the hot dog people before she ate them, or how she ate their clothes first.

I'm sure if she was sitting here now she would want to screw and eat people with Shark Girl. She might have even made little toys out of their flesh to play with before eating them. I don't think her victims would have thought she was very cute.

☺

There are things constantly moving inside of me, bubbling and millipede-crawling.

Six has them too. I see her pushing on her stomach, rubbing at things. The people inside of us are trying to regenerate, haunting our digestive system like stringy phantoms.

Nan also rubs at her stomach, but not for ghosts. She feels the baby alive inside there, twists her face and imagines what it is thinking about.

"It kind of freaks me out," she says.

"What kind of freaks you out?" I ask.

"Having something growing inside of me," she says. "It's unnatural."

"I wouldn't know," I say.

Ariel feels the woman's stomach with her little T-rex arms. "What are you talking about? It's the most natural thing in the world."

"It's disgusting," Nan says.

"Nature is usually disgusting," Ariel says.

"Nature is unnatural," Nan says.

Nan pouts at her slightly-pregnant belly.

"You're just going to throw it into the baby underground anyway," Ariel says. "You should have aborted it."

"She's not dead," I tell Ariel.

Ariel doesn't understand.

I tell her the story of Nan and Mortician coming from Earth. I tell her about The Walm and the shark people.

She doesn't understand.

"You shouldn't tell her about that," Nan tells me.

"Why not?" I ask.

"Six doesn't trust her yet," she says. "If she's loyal to The Council, you just told her about G. G. Allin's secret weapon."

"Well, it doesn't matter now," I say. "If she's one of us then she deserves to know and if she's loyal to The Council Six will just eat her. She won't be able to tell anybody after that."

Ariel doesn't make eye contact with us.

"We're going to have to tell Six about this," Nan says. "She might want to eat her just to be on the safe side."

"You know you're not helping by talking about this in front of her," I say.

Nan looks at Ariel with her baby-arms crossed at us.

"We'll just have to keep an eye on her until Six gets back," Nan says.

☺

Nan goes into the room to play with Breakfast and get some sleep, even though it's my turn to get some sleep. She's the pregnant one though, so I let her sleep.

I'm left to watch Ariel.

She wears black underwear and a black suit coat. The sleeves ripped off of the coat so she can move her arms. Her silver spiked hair has flattened to one side.

"So what happened to Sid Vicious?" I ask her.

She's thrown off by the question.

I say, "The Punk Council doesn't seem to acknowledge his existence anymore."

"He's around," she says. "He's the god of Punk Land. He's obviously around here somewhere."

"But where?" I ask.

She says, "He's busy doing godly things that we couldn't possibly understand. He wanted Johnny Rotten to take over managing the Punk government because he had more important work to do. At first, he would give messages to The Council through Johnny Rotten, but eventually Johnny Rotten took over completely."

"G. G. Allin believes Sid Vicious has been imprisoned by The Council," I say.

"I don't even know who G. G. Allin is," she says. "He probably doesn't know anything about Sid Vicious or anything about being punk."

"He takes craps on stage," I say.

"Who doesn't?" she says.

☺

Ariel is a stupid cunt.

☺

Tekky comes to my dreams again.

"You were wrong," she says.

"Wrong?" I say.

"About me and Six," she says. "We wouldn't get along. Even though she eats people."

"Why not?"

"Because she's moving in on my territory."

"What territory?"

"You," she says.

"I'm your territory?"

"She's always flirting with you."

"She is?"

"The way she feeds you, the way she always talks about biting off your head."

"I don't know how that can be considered flirting."

"She's trying to take my place as your girlfriend."

"You're my girlfriend?" I ask.

"Yeah!" she says. "We were practically married."

"We were practically strangers," I say.

"We still loved each other," she says.

"You killed me," I say.

"I killed me too!" she says.

"In any case," I say, "Six doesn't like me. I think she's more attracted to Ariel."

"She'd like to eat Ariel," Tekky says. "But she couldn't love her."

"I don't think shark girls fall in love.

They're too cold-blooded."

"They are half human," she says. "You just have to look deeper to find their emotions."

"I think you're mistaken," I say.

"I'm not saying she's in love with you yet," she says. "She would have fucked you by now if she was totally into you. I'm just saying she's getting too close. You're becoming too comfortable with her. An affection is beginning to build."

"You're imagining things," I say.

"It's like she's your provider. She goes out hunting for meat every day and then brings it home for you. She even chews your food."

"Sounds more like a child than a lover," I say.

"Yeah, but that's why there is an affection building."

"I'm a freak!"

"So is she."

"I don't get it," I say. "How can you be jealous? We hardly knew each other. You pushed me in front of a bus for fun."

"We're soul mates," she says.

"You're not even really here with me," I say. "You just haunt my dreams."

"I'm always with you," she says.

☺

I wake up.

Naked.

My arms and legs tied to a chair.

"What's going on?" I ask, my head spinning.

The room is quiet and empty. I don't
see Six anywhere. Is she finally going to
bite my head off? Maybe Nan told her what
I said to Ariel and now she wants to get
rid of me. She's going to eat me and shit
me into the sewer. Tekky was wrong about
her.

Wait a minute . . .

"You shot yourself in the foot," Ariel
says from behind.

I'm beginning to remember . . .

"I passed out . . ." I say.

She enters my vision wearing only her
black underwear.

"You gave me the perfect opportunity
for escape," she says.

She steps closer, rubbing her colorless legs at me.

"But while you're helpless," she says.
"I think I'm also going to take advantage
of you."

She removes her bra with her baby-sized
hands. Her breasts appear to be huge as she
squeezes them with those tiny fingers.

"Besides," she says, "I've never fucked
a deformed dick before."

Ariel smiles in the corner of her mouth
as she touches me. "It's all spiky and
curved. I've got to see what that feels
like."

I get hard. Nobody has touched my penis
before. Not while I was alive, not since
I've been dead. I can't help but get an
erection. Though, as deformed as I am, her
tiny little arms are the most disgusting
things I have ever seen. I really don't

want her touching me with them.

She grabs my meat mohawk with her little hands and forces my face into her tits. Her rib bones vibrate against my forehead as she groans. I'm still cloudy. Her breasts soft against my cheeks. She slips a nipple between my lips and pushes into me, drills with it until it is inside of my mouth. It tastes sweet. Sugar-coated. My tongue presses the nipple against the roof of my mouth. My lips suction against the sur-rounding skin.

"Yeah, that's it," she says, giggling.

The sweetness of her nipple begins to turn sour and tangy.

I see Breakfast waving at me from the couch. He is proud of words that have been drawn on him:

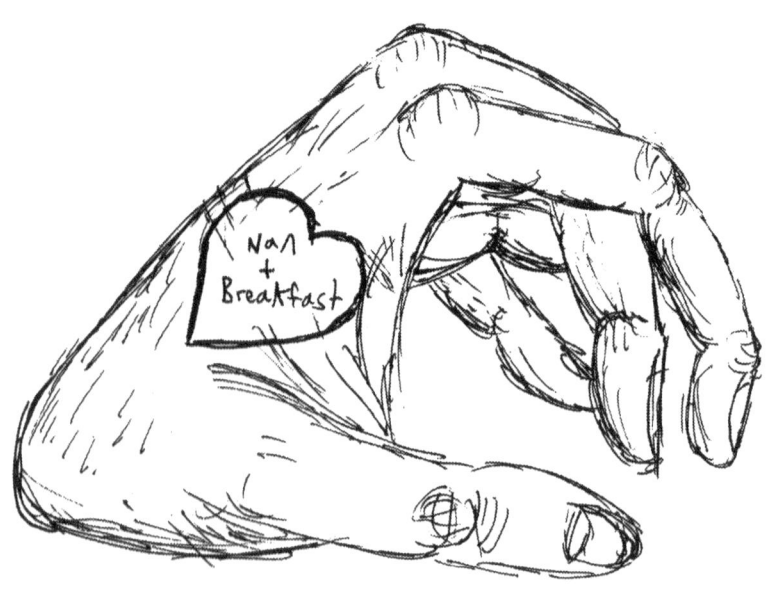

"You know, I lied to Six about why I wear a disease bikini," she says.

I try to spit out her nipple but she climbs on top of me and holds my head into place.

"I wasn't wearing it to infect Johnny Rotten," she bites her lip at me. "I wear it to infect every man I fuck."

She grinds her crotch at me, trying to slip my penis through the side of her underwear.

"Now you're infected too," she says. "You will die over and over again, for all eternity, because you fucked me."

The thought is turning her on. She gets off on diseasing people just as Six gets off on eating them. I can feel the moisture coming out of her. I'm only inches away. I don't even care that she's infected me with some horrible disease.

"The memory of me will plague your thoughts forever," she says. "You might eventually forget most of your life on Earth, but you will never forget me."

With a rolling of her hips she manages to get me inside of her, without the use of her hands. The spikes on my dick make her scream. She digs her nails into my fleshhawk so that we both feel pain.

Dropping herself up and down into my lap, screaming at me, her tiny arms dangling beside her breasts like a sexy carnivorous dinosaur . . .

Scene Seventeen
Wig Fountain

☺

Six returns a few moments too late, walking through the door with a sleeping bloody Councilman over her shoulder.

"Did she fuck you?" she asks, dropping her prisoner to untie me from the chair.

"Yeah," I say. "I've been infected."

"You're not infected," Six says. "I neutralized her disease bikini."

"How did you do that?" I ask.

"Never mind," she says. "We have to get out of here."

☺

Nan doesn't know what's happening when Six wakes her up. She doesn't remember Ariel tying her to the bed. Her sleep must have been deeper than a concentrated assihol coma.

We pull on our white jumpsuits as Six loads all the guns in the apartment. She holsters two of the guns on her thighs and carries two more. There are only five guns, so Nan and I have to share the last one. Which means I don't get a gun.

Nan holds Breakfast as if she's shaking

a severed hand.

"Leave everything else," Six tells us. "All the Co-Pos in the city are headed this way."

☺

"What about him?" I ask, pointing to the sleeping Council member on the floor.

Six steps on the man's shoulder and grabs him by the forehead. Then breaks his neck. I grind my teeth at the snapping noise.

"That'll do," she says.

He's not going to be moving for a very long time.

☺

We leave the building and head towards Pig Slut, running along the footprints and through the scorpion bubble caves.

Engines roar throughout the city, but we don't see any Co-Pos yet. They don't use sirens.

"We've probably only got five minutes before they find us," Six says.

☺

But she spoke too soon.

Ariel, wearing only black underwear and tennis shoes, comes out from behind the corner with four officers.

"There they are!" Ariel says, pointing at us with a baby arm.

Two gun shots and all four of the Co-Pos crumble to the ground.

Ariel stands there alone, dumbfounded

at Six and her two barrels pointed at her with perfect steadiness.

"Shit!" Ariel turns and jumps at the ground to dodge bullets, but no bullets are fired. Her arms aren't strong enough to catch her weight and her nose smashes against the concrete.

She gets up, looks at us, blood gushing down her neck. Then runs behind the corner.

Six just stands there.

"Let's go!" I say.

"No," the shark girl says. "We're going to follow her."

"We have to get out of here," I say.

"She's going to lead me right to their headquarters."

"Well," I say. "We're getting out of the city. You can go alone if you want."

"No," Six says. "You're safer with me."

☺

We follow Ariel.

Six can track her by scent so we don't have to stay in visual range. She won't realize we are coming after her.

Every other block, a Co-Po or two will pop out of a building in front of us, but Shark Girl shoots them in the face before they even notice us.

"Shield Nan with your body," Six says.

"Why?" I ask. "I don't want to get shot!"

"If you get shot you'll just be knocked unconscious," she says. "A bullet will kill Nan, and her baby."

I don't argue with that.

☺

Deeper into the city, the streets are filled with wigs.

Wigs of all colors and styles. I pick one up. It is curly and red.

"Where did these come from?" I ask.

"From the center of town," Six says. "I knew Council Headquarters was near Wigs Square."

☺

Closer to the city center, wigs are raining from the sky. Plopping on the ground and messing up the place. I don't know how the obsessive compulsive dictators of this city allow this litter. They cover a lot of the footprints on the sidewalk. People probably have to memorize every print, and be very careful not to trip on any of the wigs.

Then we see it: a wig fountain.

The city opens up to a large concrete park filled with steps and columns. In the middle is a lake of wigs, piles and piles of them, and at the core of the wig lake there is a wig fountain. More like a geyser that sprays dozens of wigs a mile into the air.

"What is it for?" Nan asks.

Six shrugs. "Because it's . . . punk?"

In other words: WIGS = PUNK?

???

SOME OF THE STYLES OF WIGS WE PASS:

melted
banana

chainmail locks

eyeball patch

vision pool

astro curlz

turbo volt

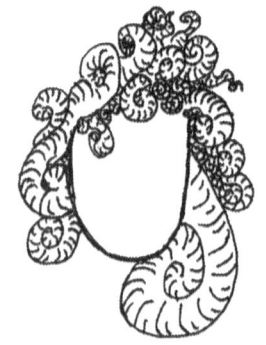

snail shells

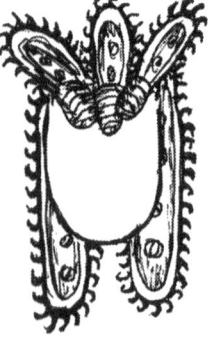

chainsaw
mullet

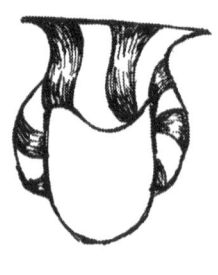

peppermint
flat top

☺

Shark Girl has lost Ariel's scent.

The wigs have covered up her trail.

Six sniffs around the perimeter of the square, but it's gone.

The mini-SUVs are getting closer.

"Six," Nan says. "We better start moving."

"Her trail is here somewhere," Six says. "We're not leaving until we know the location of the headquarters."

☺

Two SUVs come roaring into Wigs Square. They know we're the people they're looking for. Six's two-foot-tall blue mohawk gives us away. They park their vehicles in the middle of the road to create some kind of blockade.

Two more SUVs show up. Then another two. Until there are over a dozen of them. Surrounding us, guns pointed at us. An army of Co-Pos.

Too many of them, even for Shark Girl.

She lowers her guns.

Half of the officers come out from behind their vehicles, cautious-approaching.

Blank faces peek out from behind curtains in the surrounding apartment buildings.

☺

A large hatch opens within the lake of wigs.

From the darkness, men in black suits climb steps two-by-two. They march into

the square with assihol machine guns. Their
movements are perfect and precisely rhythmed.
Nazi soldier businessmen.

   And behind them, comes their gestapo,
Tick-Tock, his hands behind his back and
chin in the air. Ariel marches sloppily
next to him, wiping her bloody nose with
the S.S. officer's silk handkerchief. She
now wears an old t-shirt over her underwear that reads "What Would Johnny Rotten
Do?" in large anarchy-red lettering.

   "So that's where it was this whole time,"
Six says.

   She smiles at me, like this is all good
news.

   ☺

   "You three again," Tick-Tock says, kissing his tattooed lips at us. "You were the
ones causing the trouble all this time."

   He's unarmed. The men behind him are
his weapons. With a single word, he could
take us all down in one second.

   He pulls off his gloves to reveal:

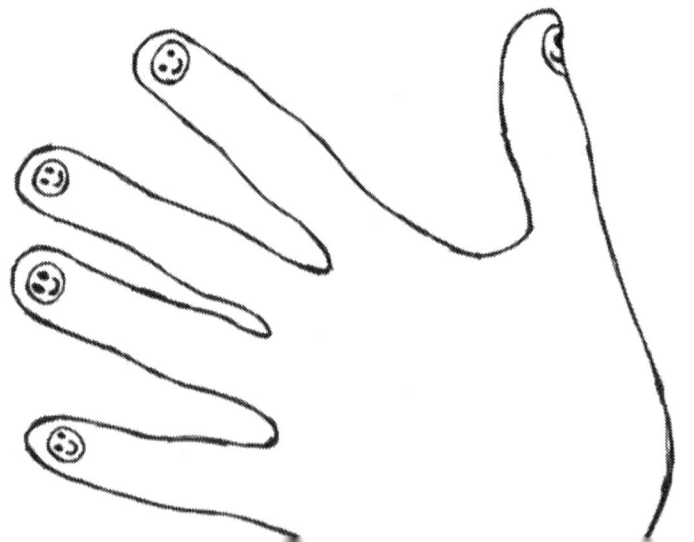

"You're going to tell me where you're keeping the kidnaped Council members," he says, stepping into Six's face. "Then you're going to explain how many more operatives God has placed in Punk Land."

Ariel steps forward, "Tick-Tock, they—"

"Your honor, please," he interrupts. "Let them speak."

Six raises her guns at the gestapo. His men raise their guns at her.

He blinks his tattooed eyelids and smiles.

"Are you going to shoot me?" he asks.

She nods.

"What is the point?" he asks. "Shoot me and my men will just shoot you. We'll all wake up later in the exact same situation. Please, don't waste our time."

Six lowers her guns.

☺

Gunshots firecracker all around me, as Nan pulls me into the lake of wigs.

Six had re-raised her guns, but instead of shooting Tick-Tock she opened fire on the suits behind him. Using the gestapo as a shield, she twists around him taking out the machine-gunners one at a time.

The Co-Pos open fire, but only hit more men in black. Tick-Tock raises his fists at them to stop. Six kicks him in the chest and he topples over, bringing several Co-Pos into view for her to shoot.

I bury myself underneath the wigs and watch through the hairs. Somehow, Breakfast managed to switch from Nan's hand to

mine. He clutches tightly around my wrist,
scared of all the gun shots fired around
us.

☺

Shark Girl's pistols are empty. She
rolls sideways over an unconscious business soldier, swiping up his machine gun
and diving into the wig lake.

I see only her blue mohawk above the
wigs as she glides across the lake and
leaps out on the other side to attack,
spraying the Co-Pos with assihol bullets.
Before the survivors can fire back, she's
already submerged, on her way to another
side of the lake. Her fin/mohawk slices
through the wigs just like water, just
like a real shark. Dipping deep below the
surface and then lunging out at them when
they least expect it.

☺

Five minutes pass.
Wigs Square quiets down.
Shark Girl rises out of the lake. Motley heads of hair dripping off her arms and
shoulders. There's only a handful of Co-
Pos left. She tosses her empty machine gun
and draws the pistols from her thigh holsters.

Casually, she shoots the last of them
one at a time. They don't fire back. Some
attempt to run away, others fall to their
knees in defeat.

Tick-Tock is tugging on a machine gun
beneath an uncommonly large sleeping/dead

officer. The strap is knotted up on the man's elbow and Tick-Tock can't get it free before Six arrives in front of him. The last of the Co-Pos on the battlefield.

"Problems?" she asks.

He kicks his feet at her and spits.

"What the hell are you?" he asks.

She kneels down and cocks her mohawk at him.

"How many more are inside?" she asks.

He tugs at the machine gun in response.

Shark Girl casually takes the gestapo's left hand and places it in her mouth. Then chews through the wrist until his hand is completely severed.

His shrieks fill the square, echo across the buildings.

The blank faces in the surrounding apartments back away from the windows. The wigs around him soak up the growing puddle of blood.

She tosses his hand aside and reveals her teeth to him, wiping his blood from the corners of her lips.

"Answer the question," she says.

Nan and I step out from beneath the wig lake, and get a good view of the bodies scattered through the streets. I try to give Breakfast back to Nan but she isn't paying attention to me.

"We're the only ones," he cries.

"If you're lying I'll bite your head off," she says. "It only takes a few seconds. You know I can do it."

He wheezes at her.

"I've heard that growing your entire

body back is an extremely painful process," she says.

"You're going to go through an eternity of pain," he says. "Once The Council's
army arrives, they'll get you. It might
take a while, but they'll get you eventually. Then you'll be mine. Forever."

"I hate to disappoint you," she tells
him. "But I'm not one of a kind. I'm just
the first. As we speak, there are hundreds
of soldiers just like me marching onto the
capital. They'll shave through your army,
through this entire city, and in the end
the entire Council will be nothing but
tiny bits on the side of the road."

Tick-Tock is busy squeezing the pain
out of his wrist.

He probably doesn't realize that he's
the only one left.

☺

We take the steps down underneath the
wig fountain.

"What happened to Ariel?" I ask.

"She escaped with a couple of suits
down here," Six replies, smelling the air.

It isn't much of a headquarters downstairs. It's more like a subway system.

There's a barracks. A few offices. An
airport-style restaurant. But it's mostly
an underground highway.

☺

"This isn't it," Six says.

Nan tips over half-finished glasses of
milk in the diner. I point a heavy machine-

gun at Tick-Tock.

"Where's Council Headquarters?" Six asks the handless gestapo.

He squirms and grinds his teeth at her.

She just has to expose her teeth to get him to talk.

"Outside of town," he says. "This tunnel will lead you to it."

"Where does it go?" she asks.

"Near the outskirts of Punk Land," he says. "To Archtopia and the military base."

"What's Archtopia?" she asks. "I've never heard of it before."

"It used to be Donkeypunchton," he says. "Until The Council took it over. It's a luxurious gated community for punk elite only."

His eyes wander, speaking to himself, "A few more years of service, and they would have let me in . . ."

Six bends over and breaks both his legs sideways. Leaving him shrieking and pounding his face into the cement, Six goes to the subway attendant station. She returns with a map of the system.

"Hey," she says, approaching Nan and Breakfast at a diner table. "We're going to Council Headquarters. I want you to take this map back to Scum Fuck and show it to Merle Allin. I've marked objectives on there for him. He'll understand. Take one of the SUVs outside and drive straight there. It should be easy to find with the map."

"Shouldn't I go to Seth Putnam first?" Nan asks.

"Fuck him," she replies. "Go straight to Scum Fuck. There might be a road block just outside of town. They're the only Co-Pos you have to worry about. Just break through and drive as fast as you can to Scum Fuck. The Co-Pos won't follow you in there."

"Got it," Nan says, saluting the shark girl with Breakfast.

"You're with me," Six tells me.

"What?" I ask. "Shouldn't I go with Nan?"

"You want to find your pet dildo don't you?" she asks.

"More than anything," I say.

"Then you better come with me," she says.

☺

Before Nan gets to the steps leading up to the wig fountain I call out to her.

"Nan."

She turns around.

"Kick some ass," I say.

She smiles at me and karate-chops the air.

☺

"We need to go, now," Six tells me. "If we don't catch up with Ariel there will be an entire army waiting for us when we get there."

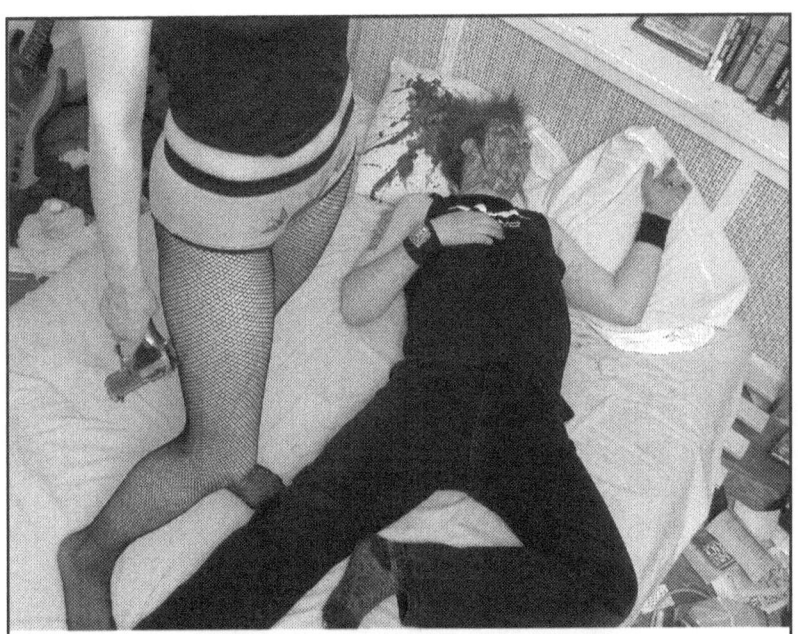

ACT THREE
THE OUTSKIRTS OF PUNK LAND

Scene Eighteen
Lung City

☺

We're within miles of Archtopia, but still no sign of Ariel.

Six drives the SUV as fast it can go through the underground tunnel. It's still not fast enough.

Tick-Tock is bleeding all over the back seat. His nice suit stained and ripped. Moaning at us.

"You'll never reach Ariel in time," he says. "The entire Council Army will be waiting for you."

"Shut up," Six tells him.

"They're not going to bother with bullets," he says. "They'll just use nerve gas. Or explosives. Don't be surprised if there's a rocket launcher waiting for us at the end of the tunnel."

"Do you want me to bite off your other hand?" Six asks.

☺

"Where will Frog Strips be?" I ask Tick-Tock.

He groans to himself.

"I've got to find Frog Strips," I say.

His voice is slurred and high-pitched, "Frog strips? What?" He sounds almost drunk now, draping his head over the back of my chair.

"He's lost a lot of blood," Six tells me.

"Now explain this," he says. "What's a Frog Strips?"

"My live dildo," I say. "I threw her at Johnny Rotten. You took her from me and dissected her . . ."

"Oh, that thing," he says. "I gave that to The Doctor."

"The Doctor?" I ask.

"That's what he calls himself."

"Like Doctor Who?" I ask.

"The hopping doctor," he says. "A lunatic, that one is."

"Where does he keep Frog Strips?" I ask.

"I don't have a clue," he says. "His lab, I'd guess. I've never been allowed in there."

"Where's his lab?"

"In the new headquarters building," he says.

"Where's that?"

"We'll be there within minutes."

"Where—"

Six cuts me off.

"Stop asking him questions," she says. I sink into my seat.

"There might not even be time to look for your dildo," she says.

"But you said . . ."

"I'm not going to guarantee you anything," she says. "If I'm able to take out The Council and secure the facility, we'll have time to look for Frog Strips while we wait for backup to arrive. Otherwise you'll have to wait until after we've won the war."

"We must get her back now!" I say.

"Don't worry," she says. "The war should be over within days."

☺

There are bright lights up ahead.

"Is that it?" Six asks Tick-Tock.

"That's it," he says. "Council Headquarters."

Six turns off the lights and pulls over.

"Ariel must have made it," I say.

"She must have," Six says. "But they're not ready for us."

"Probably didn't think you had the balls to follow her," says Tick-Tock.

"That's exactly what I wanted her to think," says the shark girl.

☺

We sit in the darkness for awhile, adjusting our eyes.

Six turns her head to Tick-Tock.

"You're coming with us," she says, soft-voiced.

He groans at her. "How am I supposed to go? You broke both my legs."

"I'm sorry," she says, "but we're going to have to leave most of you behind."

"Leave most of me behind?" he asks, pondering her words, eyes wandering the roof of the SUV.

He doesn't see it coming. Not paying attention at all as she leans in and wraps her teeth around his throat. She bites through the voice box first so that he can't scream, then chews around the throat and snaps the spine off at the skull.

His headless body noodles back in the seat, as blood fountains out of his neck in thick boogery chunks.

☺

Walking through the tunnel with Tick-Tock's head wrapped in his coat and tied to Shark Girl's waist:

"Why are we taking his head?" I whisper-ask.

"We might need directions," she says.

"But he doesn't have a throat or lungs anymore," I say. "He's not able to talk."

"He can still communicate non-verbally," she says. "Besides, we don't want him making noise."

I ask, "Isn't he going to leave a long bloody trail behind us?"

"He's mostly out of blood," she says.

☺

Six doesn't work as stealthily as I thought she would.

We walk out of the darkness and she shoots five guards. All of them in valet uniforms.

"Where's Ariel?" I ask.

"She didn't stop here." Six smells the metal doors that lead into Council Headquarters, smells the sidewalks, and the valet uniforms. "She must have continued on."

"This is the headquarters, isn't it?" I ask.

"I think she went straight to the military base," she says. "I don't think she even stopped to warn the guards. They don't have her smell."

☺

Inside the building, we are attacked by colors. Like a space-aged casino mixed with a children's play park, lights and sounds are flashing all around us, splashes of bright colors move across the walls, rainbows swirl in the carpeting beneath our feet.

It is the complete opposite of the capital. Instead of a haunted dreary place, it is filled with animation and happiness. Blue and pink cocktails in tubular glasses. Three-dimensional television shows featuring breakdancing ninjas. Water slides. Bubble machines. Dancing robot strippers with laser guns.

"What is this place?" I ask Six, yelling loud enough so she can hear over the laserbeam noises. "I thought this was supposed to be Council Headquarters?"

She responds but I can't hear what she says. I just follow her.

The room is probably a square mile. There aren't many people in here, but it feels crowded. There are a few valet guards along the walls but they don't seem to recognize us. Even with Shark Girl's two foot mohawk.

We pass a businessman sitting in a booth with a naked robot dancing for him on a table, rolling her mechanical hips and clank-smacking her ass. She's teasing him with shiny lips and shooting him in the chest with her laser gun as he masturbates. His body filled with charred holes and he begs her to shoot him some more.

Six halts in front of me and I collide with her back, too distracted to pay attention to where she's leading me. She fires her gun at guards ahead of us. The partying businessmen don't notice. I peek over her shoulder and see two fallen guards near an elevator. They probably didn't even see us before they were hit. We drag them into a nearby hot tub filled with floating rubber turtles.

Nobody sees us. Nobody is watching.

☺

In the elevator, Six takes Tick-Tock's head off of her waist and out of the coat.

His face is soggy with pain and crunchy with blood.

"Where are the Council offices?" she asks him as if he can talk.

His mouth is dangled open. He can hardly keep his tongue in his mouth, let alone speak. The only thing he can move is his eyes as they attempt to look away from us.

"Blink when I point to the right floor," she says.

He closes his eyes.

ROBOT STRIPPER RULES

1) Do not attempt to have sex with the robot stripper.

2) No jerking off onto the robot stripper.

3) Only one robot stripper per customer.

4) Do not proposition the robot stripper to shoot you or other patrons with their laser guns.

5) Management is not responsible for laser damage caused by the robot stripper.

6) Management is not responsible for lost appendages caused from attempting to fornicate with the robot stripper.

7) Do not attempt to reprogram the robot stripper.

8) Remain fully clothed for the duration of all lap dances.

9) If the credit card slot on the back of the robot stripper is out of order, please notify security and move to the next stripping station.

10) Robot strippers have the right to deny lap dances to excessively sweaty patrons.

"Not going to help?" she asks. "Don't think things can get any worse?"

He doesn't open his eyes.

"I can suck the skin off your face," she says. "Or I can crush your skull under my heel."

He opens his eyes, but Six still drops him on the floor. Presses against his face with her Grinders. She scrunches her lips at me as she applies weight to her foot.

"It takes just a second to stomp your head into a chunky mess," she says to him. "That's the first thing I will do if you lead us astray."

She retrieves him from the floor, his black-veined eyes wide open, and holds him by the neck in front of the elevator buttons.

He blinks his tattooed eyelids when she points to the 28th floor.

"All the way to the top," she says.

On the way up, I use the same process to ask him what level Frog Strips will be on.

His eyes blink yes when I ask him if he knows what floor the lab is on, but he doesn't blink on any of the buttons as I point to them. He blinks three times after I stop pointing at the buttons, but I don't know what he's trying to say.

☺

The elevator has a window so that we can look out over the city of Archtopia. If you can call it a city. It isn't the upper class suburban community I was picturing. It's a grotesque future world of white rubber and purple steam.

The Archtopian homes are not solid brick and mortar buildings, they are stretchy rubber pulsating blobs. They slowly balloon inwards and outwards, as if the houses were breathing, like they are not houses, but lungs. Their doors and windows are as they should be, they have lawns and white picket fences, but their exteriors appear to be human tissue.

"How did they build this so fast?" I ask.

Six doesn't comment.

"This was just a tiny village a couple years ago," I say.

Tick-Tock's eyes are wide at the city, entranced by it. He said The Council was going to let him live in this community after a few more years of service, but now he sees his dreams slipping away from him. He's just a head now. Even if Six fails to overthrow The Council, he'll still be a head until his body grows back. They'll probably have to fire him or demote him for unleashing a shark girl onto Council Headquarters. Either way, he's probably never going to get to live inside a lung or get shot with lasers by a robot stripper, ever.

☺

When we reach the top floor, I cower into a corner of the elevator away from the door, getting out of Six's way as she charges in, guns blazing.

This time she doesn't look out for me.

She just runs off, leaves me behind in the elevator. I hear gun shots reverberating throughout the 28th floor, even more shooting than in Wigs Square, and it fades to a quiet popping as she charges farther and farther away from me.

I am all alone.

The elevator door opens and closes, opens and closes. It is Tick-Tock's head in the doorway, propped there, that keeps the elevator from moving.

I peek out from behind the opening/closing door: a wide open lobby painted to look like the cosmos, blue planet-shaped furniture, the Milky Way for a ceiling.

The floor is mirror-tiled to reflect the walls, making it feel as if the room stretches forever in every direction. Dozens of bloody suited guards lie across the tiles. They look like they are floating in outer space.

I exit the elevator and replace Tick-Tock's head with a swirly red pillow from a lobby couch, carrying him a foot ahead of me, his ears like tiny handles. It feels as if there isn't a floor as I walk across to the other side, pretending the head in my hands is just a deflated basketball.

Through black curtains is a regular hallway. Kind of white and sterile like a hospital, but normal enough for me to get through without going dizzy.

I take every step with caution. It is mostly silent besides the whir of computers and coffee machines. Not as many bodies to step over, but there are some. All of the doors along the hall lead to large offices, each containing a folded-over businessman or woman filled with bullets. She must have gone room to room, shooting them one at a time.

Farther down, the bodies are much more messy. People missing their arms and legs, heads torn from necks, spines ripped out of backs. One woman has even been ripped in half, vertically. These bodies weren't hit with assihol, so they are still conscious, twitching and gurgling at me.

☺

I catch up to Shark Girl. Near the end of the hallway, I see her through a set of windows inside of a boardroom. She is standing on the table, pointing a bloody samurai sword at the people gathered around her. She must have interrupted some kind of business meeting, crashed in and took them all hostage. Where she got the samurai sword, I have no idea. Perhaps there's a sword display in one of the offices. In any case, it suits her.

She's a punk rock ninja shark chick.

I can't hear what she's saying through the sound-proof glass, but she is shouting and swinging blood at their faces. A few of the businessmen are missing their heads. Most of them frozen, in complete shock. They never expected this to happen.

☺

I try to open the doors, but they have been barricaded from the other side. Six doesn't want any of them getting out. When I wiggle the doorknob, everybody turns to me. They look at me with their cold grumpy faces.

Wait a minute . . .

They are . . . *old*.

Very old.

What are all these rich elderly conservative men doing in Punk Land?

How did they get in?

I worked at the gates. They never would have been allowed in. Even a clueless idiot like me, who had no place as an authority on punk, would ever have let them in.

And *they* are The Council?

They are the people in charge of Punk Land?

Six is breathing heavily, staring at me with her reddened face, communicating to me with her eyes all of the hate and disgust that she feels right now. Not only for The Council, but for all of Punk Land.

She waves me away. She doesn't want me to see what she's about to do to them.

If it's any uglier than what she usually does to people, then I really don't want to see it.

☺

I wander to the end of the hall, checking to see if there's anybody else around. There's a security station filled with keys and monitors, but it has been abandoned. Tick-Tock's head squirts a grey fluid as I set it on top of one of the monitors to search the desk for a gun.

There is one but I can't find any extra bullets for it.

Tick-Tock's grey fluids are leaking down the screen of a monitor and puddling on the keyboard in front of me.

"You made a mess," I say to the head, wiping the mucous with my sleeve.

His eyes roll back, tongue bulging out at me.

On the screen, there are white-mohawked army men charging through a tunnel. Another screen shows the white-mohawked men pushing robotic strippers out of their way. Another screen shows them charging up a staircase.

☺

I take Tick-Tock out of the room and go to tell Six about the army men, but she is already on her way to the lobby.

She stops when she sees me, "We need to hold them off for as long as possible!" Then continues on.

I look into the boardroom windows, can hardly see through all the blood on the glass. There's not much left of the people inside. It's as if Six liquified them in a giant blender. And then the blender exploded.

"What did you do to The Council?" I ask.

She stops at the end of the lobby, turns around.

"They're not The Council," she responds. "They are The Executives. They're the ones who really run Punk Land. Johnny Rotten, the Punk Council, Mosh City, it's all a front."

I raise Tick-Tock's head to eye level to see if she's telling the truth and he blinks.

"Come on," Six tells me. "We need to barricade the door to the stairway."

Scene Nineteen
The Hopping Doctor

☺

While checking the offices for barricading supplies, I come to another stairwell. Not the one Six is laboring over, a different one.

"We've got two," I call out to the shark girl but she's too far away.

I open the door and listen for footsteps, but the steps don't go down. They go up. Looking up the stairs, I see at least five more stories. Maybe more.

"This isn't the top floor?" I ask Tick-Tock's head.

The head blinks.

"Do you think The Doctor's lab is up there?" I ask.

The head blinks.

"I bet Frog Strips is up there somewhere," I say.

The head blinks.

"I'll have to check it out."

The head blinks.

☺

Up the steps and to the first door. My gun in one hand, Tick-Tock's head in the other.

I peek through the little window on the door.

It is one large room. Dimly lit. There are rows and rows of large shelves that reach all the way to the ceiling. A kind of library or file room. My breath creates a frost on the glass and I can no longer see within. I put Tick-Tock's head in my armpit and open the door with my pinkies.

It is a freezer.

Entering just a few feet, I get a closer look at the shelves: bodies.

Aisle after aisle of frozen punks, within thick blocks of ice and filed away where they'll never be seen again. There must be thousands of them in here. All the people who ran out of punk points, all the people who couldn't fit in. All the *real* punks.

They all ended up here.

☺

The next floor is another freezer storage. So are the next five.

Half the population of Punk Land must be up here, locked away so that The Executives don't have to deal with them.

How did The Executives come to Punk Land anyway? Through The Walm like Nan and Mortician? Did a gate attendant sneak them through? Or maybe they don't really have souls and are just a product of Sid Vicious' nightmare subconscious, like the corpses in the catacombs or the pizza cats or the underground neighborhood.

They've made this place worse than

Heaven. We have to put a stop to it now. If Six can somehow cut the power to these floors all of these punks would defrost. We'd have an army ten times the size of The Council Army, with Six and Frog Strips leading the way.

☺

The lab is at the very top.

Tick-Tock closes his eyes shut tight when I look through the little window on the door.

This room also has frozen bodies, but not too many. Probably just a hundred or so. The majority of the space is filled with electronic equipment shaped like enormous snails. The floor is a mess of wires and thick tubes. Fans and rubber balloons dangle from the ceiling.

There are three men in the room. Two are lying naked on tables, and the third standing above them. Two unconscious patients and a doctor. One patient is female and appears to be recently thawed. The standing doctor is wearing a white leather lab coat and has very long stilt-like legs. He's probably 12 feet tall and he has to squat down to reach his patients, his knees over the top of his head.

With multi-jointed elbows the doctor bends his arm backwards to plug the half-frozen female into one of the snail-shaped machines. The other patient, a cleanly shaved male, is already full of plugs. Half of his body seems interwoven into the computers.

"Could it be?" I say to myself. "Is it Him?"

Tick-Tock opens his eyes for a second and then closes them again. A reverse blink.

The shaved half-electronic man . . .

It's Sid Vicious.

☺

He's here.

Right here in front of me.

All I have to do is enter the room and point my gun at this crazy doctor. Demand him to release Frog Strips and Sid Vicious. Take them to safety.

Punk Land is His world. He can retake it with ease.

He can bring back the anarchy utopia.

And everything would be good forever and ever.

But my hands won't open the door. My feet don't want to enter.

Even Tick-Tock's head refuses to open its eyes.

☺

The Doctor turns on the snail machine and clicks at buttons and levers on a control panel. The woman's body heats to a green glow and she begins to deflate. The machine absorbs her. Just a little at a time. It's sucking her up like fuel, using her lifeforce as a battery.

The electronics on Sid Vicious glow red. They zap and vibrate him. He cries out in his sleep. Like bad dreams ripping through his mind.

THE DOCTOR'S MACHINE:

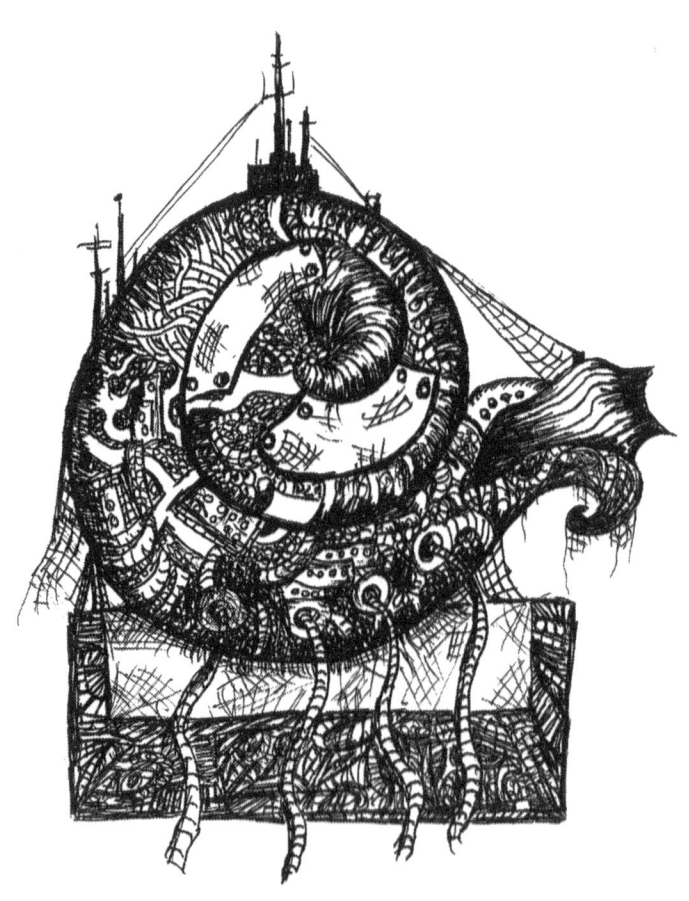

Something is forming out of thin air behind them. A brownish blob. The Doctor watches carefully, adjusting his controls as it forms. It's like he's drawing a picture with the levers, and the picture is becoming reality.

The blob solidifies into a black humanoid creature with metal skin. A mechanical demon.

"Finally . . ." The Doctor says, a deep dragon's voice.

☺

Six enters the stairwell shouting.

"Goblin?" she cries. "Are you in here?"

The Doctor hears her. He turns his head and sees me in the window. His eyes are tiny doorknobs. His mouth filled with wire mesh instead of teeth.

"Goblin!" she calls again.

I run down the stairs.

"I'm coming!" I cry.

There's no way I'm facing The Doctor without Shark Girl.

☺

"We need to get out of here, now," she says. Her voice almost happy and excited.

"But, upstairs—" I say.

"Never mind that now," she says. "We'll come back."

She's carrying a garbage bag over her shoulder. Probably containing all the heads or the brains of The Executives, so that they don't regenerate after we're gone.

"How are we going to get out of here?"

I ask.

"Elevator," she says.

☺

Council soldiers try to break through her barricade of couches and desks and security guards as we take the elevator down to the lobby.

"This is going to be fun," Six tells me, cocking her mohawk from side to side.

"What?" I ask.

"You'll see," she says.

☺

The elevator doors open to a raging battle within the futuristic night club.

We are behind a row of white-mohawked soldiers firing into the colorful casino world, missing their targets and hitting all the robot strippers and masturbating businessmen. Their targets move swiftly, swimming through the shadows of the multi-colored lights.

"They're here?" I ask.

Six's smile is so BIG I can see all the rows of her teeth.

☺

Dozens of Asian shark people leap out of the darkness to attack the Council soldiers. They are all Mortician's offspring, but are more like clones than children. They share his exact memories, think as he would think, but can fight like Shark Girl.

Wearing pirate outfits, the young shark people lunge forward with a new type of weapon: nets made of razor-strings. They swing the nets at their enemy and the nets cut through the flesh and bone like cheese, dicing them into pieces with a single strike.

All around us, the shark pirates dart through the crowd of army men, leaving the soldiers in small chunks as they pass.

"My family!" Six says to me, very proud of her younger brothers and sisters. "Aren't they wonderful?"

I nod at her.

"Let's go!" she says.

And Six raises her sword, charging toward the men in front of us, to attack them from behind.

☺

I wander aimlessly through the battle.

All of the shark people know who I am so I don't get diced as I walk. A soldier turns to shoot me, but he crumbles to pieces with a snap. Another explodes into confetti just for looking at me. Their screams linger in the air after they've gone. I barely see my Asian shark girl protector as she swims by.

I look at Tick-Tock's head. His tattooed eyelids are wobbling shut as if this all bores him to tears.

☺

Ariel is here!

She's standing in the middle of a crowd of businessmen with machine guns. Tick-Tock's men. Now she's wearing army pants and a muscle-shirt, though her baby arms look really out of place dangling out of the muscle shirt.

"Over there!" she cries when she sees me. "Get him."

The businessmen don't listen to her, though. Too busy getting picked off one by one. The shark pirates circling them like wounded prey as Ariel punches the air with her tiny fists.

☺

Six catches up with me as the last of Ariel's men falls.

"You fucking bitch!" Ariel screams at Six.

A shark Mortician steps behind the silver-spiked woman and stretches his razor-net weapon out above her. I get a better look at the weapon. It has handles on each end. Looks kind of like a personal-sized volleyball net. They wear chainmail gloves on their hands to prevent cuts. The razor strands glisten in the disco lighting.

Very slowly, as if he knows Six wants to savor the moment, the shark guy lowers the net down on Ariel cranium-first like he's zipping down a raincoat. She breathes fast and heavy, I can hear her skin tearing over the battle sounds around us, sweat pouring down her bony shoulders. But she does not scream.

After the net reaches her feet, she continues panting and sweating until her heavy breathing causes her to fall apart. The strands of her body fold in opposite directions, blooming open like a flower and collapsing into twitchy noodles on the floor.

A potato that's been turned into french fries.

☺

A shower of bullets tear through the shark guy standing over Ariel's pieces.

He dies before hitting the ground.

We look behind us and see the black mechanical demon from upstairs. Its arms have heavy machine guns built into the wrists. Shark people swipe past him, but their razor nets cannot cut through its metal skin.

The demon opens fire on the room and takes down both sharks and soldiers alike.

"We better not stick around," Six says, pushing me to the exit.

Her younger brothers and sisters gang up on the demon, circling him. They can't cut through his armor, but they are quick enough to dodge his bullets as they search for a weak point.

☺

Two shark people flee with us, out of the exit into the underground highway. There are half a dozen soldiers out here but they are unarmed. They raise their hands as if to surrender. One of the shark pirates passes Six and picks out a mini-SUV for us, opens the door and gets in the driver's seat.

"We did it," Six tells me, raising the bag of old man pieces.

Tick-Tock is missing an eye.

I want to get into the vehicle but Six is blocking my way. Her smile is falling from her face at something over my shoulder.

Before Six can push me out of the way, a bullet breaks open the back of my skull and fills my brain with battery acid. I drop into her arms, my forehead landing on her chin, everything getting fizzy.

Scene Twenty
Vaginas With Vampire Fangs

☺

I wake up.

Stretching and groaning out of sleep. Nauseous and the back of my head throbbing.

I'm wearing a white gown with a bandage around my skull, in a small room with two empty beds and a couple apricot dressers.

A nurse in white latex and spiky platinum hair passes by and sees me sitting up in bed, trying not to puke.

"He's awake," she says to somebody behind me, and continues on.

"Hey! Goblin!" I hear some guy call out in a party dude voice.

He comes around the corner and enters the room. "What's going on?"

I don't recognize him. Some deformed guy holding an assihol beer.

Wait a minute ...

"Grak?" I ask.

"Hey, hey," Grak says.

☺

It's Grak. My best friend, my punk family. The guy I came from Heaven with. The friend I lost after he was stabbed by an angry skinhead.

"What are you doing here?" I ask.

"I live here," he says.

"Where are we?"

"The home of the dead," he says. "You died, guy. Remember? Killed in the revolution."

"But the other Punk Council stopped playing by those rules," I say. "I thought they shut this place down."

"Nope," he says, offering me a beer but I wave it back. "This place isn't within Council territory. It's under the control of The New Order."

"The New Order?" I ask. "Is that a new government?"

"No, it's kind of a code of honor out here," he says. "I'll have to tell you about it later."

"Where's Shark Girl?" I ask. "Where are my other friends?"

"They only brought one other guy in with you, the one that was just a head. He's over in the intensive recovery area. They're keeping him sedated with assihol so that he doesn't have to go through the pain. They did that to you as well."

"How long have I been out?" I ask.

"A few weeks," he says.

"So Six got away?" I ask. "What happened?"

"I don't know," he says. "You're the latest addition to our community so you know more about the outside world than anyone else. All I know is that G. G.

Allin's people had you sent here, because you've been killed."

"You don't know about The Executives yet? Or Sid Vicious? Or Archtopia?" I ask.

"You can tell me about it later," he says. "Everybody here is going to have a million questions for you. You should get some rest before the *interrogation* begins."

"Sounds like fun," I say.

"You won't be saying that after telling a hundred people the same story over and over again," he says, laughing. "Believe me, it's pretty annoying."

"Maybe I should write it all down and make copies to pass out to everyone," I say.

"Hey, that's a good idea," he says. "Maybe you should. They have a copy machine here. But we mostly just use it to copy our butts."

"So what do I do here?" I ask. "We just hang out in this place while the war is going on out there?"

"Got no choice," he says. "You're dead. Can't help them now."

"But the people they are fighting don't die," I say.

"Just because they cheat doesn't mean you should too," he says.

He finishes the beer and leaves it on the floor.

"Look," he says. "I've got to get back to work. I'm on laundry duty. Your roommate should be back any minute, if you have any questions."

"Roommate?" I ask.

M.U.S.C.L.E.

(Millions of Unusual Small Creatures Lurking Everywhere)

These tiny pink action figures are laid out
on top of one of the dressers in this room.

"Yeah," he says. "She insisted on sharing a room with you. Some new girl. I think you know her. Her name's Teri or something like that."

"Tekky?" I ask.

"Yeah," he says. "That's her."

"She's here?" I ask. "In the flesh?"

"Yeah. Weird girl. Cute though. Well, I better leave you to it. Get some rest. We'll talk later."

"See ya," I say and lie back into the bed.

Tekky?

She's really here?

☺

Sure enough, I'm re-united with Tekky when she jumps onto the bed and hops up and down on my legs.

"You're dead!" she cries with glee. "Yay!"

Then she lies down next to me, her crusty hair against my hand. "Isn't it great?"

"How did you get here?" I ask.

"I died too," she says.

"I mean, how did you find me?" I ask.

"I told you last time," she says. "We're soulmates."

"Last time?" I ask.

"Just a few weeks ago," she says.

"That was a dream," I say.

"So," she says.

"It was just in my head," I say. "It wasn't real."

"But I came from your head," she says.

"I know how to go in and out whenever I want. You know that."

"What are you talking about?" I ask.

"When I was imaginary, on Earth," she says.

"I don't understand," I say.

"You never knew? I thought for sure you knew!" she says.

"What?"

"Back on Earth, we lived in the same body," she says. "Nobody could see me except you."

"What are you saying? You were some kind of split personality? An imaginary friend."

"Kind of both, but more than that," she says. "I'm your feminine side made flesh. I'm your soulmate. Or perhaps your body mate."

My eyebrows curl at her. She can tell this needs more explaining.

"Twins are born when an egg divides into two," she says. "In our case, the soul inside your body was divided into two. We are soul twins. Since we shared a brain, our thoughts were mostly combined. But eventually I was able to separate us and let us develop individually."

"But you used to eat my cereal, cut yourself, you pushed me in front of a bus!"

"All done with the same body," she says. "It was kind of neat and cosy to be trapped in the same shell with you, but I killed our body so that our spirits could be free, and we could be together as a real couple in the afterlife. Unfortunately, you were so angry with me that you left me back on Earth and went to Heaven. I was all alone. Luckily I found Punk Land."

"Why didn't you come to me sooner?" I ask.

"Oh, I've been busy!" she says. "With my artwork!"

She sits up on the bed and raises her fists at the mightiness of artwork.

"Besides, it was easy enough to be with you in our dreams," she says. "Our dreams are connected no matter how far away we are from each other."

"I thought I was crazy," I say.

"Well, you're definitely weird," she says. "But you were never crazy."

☺

Days pass.

Tekky and I are in love. We are able to have real sex now. We don't have to try to cut ourselves while masturbating within the same body.

Word spreads about our history, how we divided from the same soul and became lovers, and we become a sort of curiosity around the home of the dead. Everybody always has questions for us, either about our relationship or about the current affairs of Punk Land. I decided to create a newsletter using the copy machine in the nurse's station, explaining the whole state of Punk Land.

It's so popular among the punks that Tekky and I plan to start The Dead Times, a local community newspaper. We'll be interviewing the new dead people and getting the latest news on the world outside. Tekky wants to illustrate it, but I'm not sure if people will like a bunch of drawings of vaginas.

"But I've created a new series even better than the last!" she cries.

She shows me a new series of drawings. Instead of vaginas eating fairies, they are all vaginas with vampire fangs. She shows them to me and then opens her mouth and hisses at me like a vampire. Some of them show the vaginas drinking blood from their victims' necks, some drawings feature vaginas swooping down from the sky at people, some wear black skirts like a Dracula cape.

"These are wonderful!" I tell her. "Your best work yet!"

And I almost mean it this time.

☺

Tekky is up in our room drawing pictures for the first issue of The Dead Times.

I'm out in the courtyard with Grak. We've hardly had much time to talk since I've been here. Tekky doesn't really like to share my company with others.

"It's not bad," I tell him. "Living here like this."

"Yeah," he says. "It's not bad at all. We'll be here for ten years, though. Might get boring later on, but we try to keep each other entertained."

"What do you think you'll do after you leave?" I ask.

"Depends on the state of the government. If The Council has fallen, I'll probably visit the different cities, see what's changed since I've been gone. If The Council still controls the place, I'll be heading farther into the wilds."

"What's out there?" I ask.

"There's endless possibilities out there," he says. "Even if The Council takes over the heart of Punk Land, we can all create new societies deeper into the wilds. Punk Land is limitless. It goes on forever. If Sid Vicious' imagination doesn't create the land for us, then the land will mutate to suit our own imaginations. We can be like the gods of our own worlds out there."

"Why don't you do that now?" I ask. "Why not escape and go past the outskirts of Punk Land?"

"I could," he says. "There aren't any guards here anymore."

"No guards?" I ask. "Then what's holding you back?"

"The New Order," he says.

He stretches his back and opens another beer. "You don't know about The New Order yet, right?"

I shrug.

"It's the anarchy utopia," he says. "Anarchy is the only true freedom. Under any kind of government, we are prisoners. But anarchy can create chaos, and dictators then come into power to bring order to the chaos. Many people are willing to sacrifice freedom for order."

"Which is why The Council was able to come into power?" I ask.

"The New Order is about self-government and maturity. Compare a government and its citizens to parents and their children. Before maturity, kids are undisciplined. They are given laws for their own good, because they don't know any better. Once the children grow up, they become independent. They make their own rules. They're mature enough to discipline themselves. But the problem with our society is that we are still like kids. Our civilization hasn't grown up enough to take care of ourselves. We need rules and we need people to enforce the rules. Bringing anarchy to a society like that is like giving complete freedom to six-year-olds and allowing them to do whatever they want. They don't know what's best for them, just as individuals don't know what's best for their community."

"But that means anarchy is a hopeless system," I say. "If just one citizen refuses to play fair, then it won't work."

"The New Order is about education," he continues. "Education breeds maturity, and maturity breeds self-government. We have to help each other understand the importance of protecting the individual. Every person is their own country, their own government."

"But not everybody has the same morals. What is right for some people is wrong for others."

"The highest ideal in the code of honor

is to respect one another's individuality. True open-mindedness is the most admirable and virtuous quality a human being can have. It isn't love, it isn't charity, it is respect and understanding. The ideas of right and wrong, good and evil, all promote close-mindedness. People must know those terms are subjective, only opinions."

"But you would still have to enforce rules to keep people open-minded. Not everybody will realize it is more important than being right."

"Eventually they will learn," he says. "The lesson will be repeated until it is learned. Perhaps we do need a government during the education process, but the main goal of the government should be working towards diminishing itself. Giving as many freedoms to the people as they can handle. Then educating them on aspects they can't handle until they can handle it again."

"I don't know," I tell him. "Sounds like an impossible goal."

"But one that is worthy of pursuit," he says.

"I think it's a bit futile," I say. "The only way we can be free is if we are free of each other."

"It's really not hopeless, Goblin," he says. "It is the future of civilization."

☺

One night, Six comes to my bedroom.

I'm not sure if it's a dream or reality.

She wakes me up and asks me to leave

with her, that the revolution needs my help.

But I don't go.

"I'm dead," I tell her. "I must stay here."

She continues to persuade me, cocking her blue mohawk at me and squeezing my arm tight, but I will not leave.

I must play fair.

But did I stay to play fair or did I stay because I like it here?

I wonder if I would have agreed to go if I wasn't so happy in this place. If all of my friends and Tekky were out there in the world living their lives as I rotted here pretending to be dead, would I stay here just out of principle? Sure, life with the possibility of death makes living more fun and exciting, but is it worth sacrificing my happiness? It isn't fun to pretend to die when playing war on the playground, but if you don't do it you'll ruin the game.

Perhaps if I thought of the others play-ing the game instead of myself I might be more contempt to play fair . . .

☺

I fall back into sleep, Tekky wrapped around me like I'm her body pillow, her hair cinnamon-flavored against my lips.

I dream that the punk rebels attack Archtopia one more time.

I dream of Six freeing Sid Vicious from the hopping doctor. Shark pirates racing through Lung City taking down black mechanical demons, Seth Putnam and Johnny Thunderpants drink assihol in the background, making fun of everyone for fighting in a war.

I dream The Council is overthrown. G. G. Allin beats the crap out of Johnny Rotten. All of the frozen punks escape from Council Headquarters and graffiti rampage through the streets of the capital.

In another town, I see Nan give birth to a baby boy. Breakfast holds her hand during the labor. She decides to name the child Gin.

Mortician is killed by one of the sharks he's been mating with. He dies and then is reborn again. Merle Allin tells him that his services are no longer needed and that he should go to the home for the dead.

I see a new world without government. Sid Vicious steps back and allows the society to grow without a leader.

In the home for the dead, I'm outside lounging on the lawn with Tekky and Mortician, drinking cocktails and discussing future articles for The Dead Times.

Grak is under a tree, writing his utopian manifesto.

Tekky bounces Tick-Tock's head on her knee like a baby.

And from the distance, I see Six and Nan, coming to tell us that they killed themselves to be with us. Nan carrying Breakfast and Gin. Six with her new shark boyfriend, carrying a large blue box.

When they arrive to us, Six smiles with all of her rows of teeth and hands me the blue box.

"It's a present!" she says.

I already know what it is before I open it. It's Frog Strips!

Sitting inside the box with a little bow around her neck. The permanent bruise on her neck has miraculously healed.

I pick up my baby and cradle her in my arms. All of my friends come to see. They smile with glee at Frog Strips, petting her back, clapping their hands in excitement.

Tekky gives her a BIG kiss.

"Our cute baby!" she cries.

And for the rest of the afternoon, we huddle around the box like a campfire, basking in the bliss of the dildo.

THE   END

ABOUT THE AUTHOR

Carlton Mellick III is one of the leading names in the new BIZARRO genre uprising. In only a few short years, his surreal counterculture novels have drawn an international cult following despite the fact that they have been shunned by most libraries and corporate bookstores. His work has appeared in over 100 magaiznes and anthologies, including Random Acts of Weirdness, Tempting Disaster, and The Year's Best Fantasy and Horror 16.

He sings for a band called "Popes That Are Porn Stars" in Portland, OR.

Visit him online at: **www.avantpunk.com**

ABOUT THE COVER ARTIST

Kyle Cassidy is a video artist and freelance writer who works for the Annenberg School for Communication in Philadelphia. He is also instigator of the picture a week ("paw") project.

View his online portfolio at: **www.kylecassidy.com**

ABOUT THE COVER MODEL

Darenzia is New York City's premiere fetish model, appearing in publications such as Skin Two, Marquis, Heavy Rubber, Leg Show & on the cover of Secret Magazine. She is also a performer, pro-domme, and journalist.

Visit her online at: **www.darenzia.net**

BIZARRO

A new genre of film and literature.

For eons, people have been going into bookstores and video stores looking for the weird stuff. To them, "weird stuff" is a genre, just like horror or science-fiction. But it has never been given an official name before. Until now.

Bizarro directors: David Lynch, Alexandro Jodorowsky, Brothers Quay, Jan Svankmajer, Takashi Miike, Shinya Tsukamoto, Lloyd Kaufman, John Waters, among others.

Bizarro authors: Steve Aylett (steveaylett.com), Kenji Siratori (kenjisiratori.com), Carlton Mellick III (avantpunk.com), Chris Genoa (chrisgenoa.com), D. Harlan Wilson (dharlanwilson.com), Andre Duza, (houseofduza.com), Jeremy Robert Johnson (jeremyrobertjohnson.com), John Edward Lawson (johnlawson.org), Kevin L. Donihe, Mike Philbin, Alyssa Sturgill, among others.

Bizarro publishers: Raw Dog Screaming Press, Afterbirth Books, Eraserhead Press, Skull Vomit Press, among others.

Coming in 2006: www.bizarrogenre.org

Books by Carlton Mellick III
www.AVANTPUNK.com

As an underground author, Carlton Mellick III's books can only be special ordered at local bookstores or purchased through online retailers such as www.amazon.com. If you'd like this to change, please ask your bookstores and libraries to carry future CM3 books.

Satan Burger

Satan Burger

a novel by Carlton Mellick III

TEETH AND TONGUE LANDSCAPE

a novel by Carlton Mellick III
illustrated by Brian Doogan

OCEAN OF LARD

by KEVIN L. DONIHE and CARLTON MELLICK III

ILLUSTRATED by TERRASA ULM

THE BABY JESUS BUTT PLUG

A FAIRY TALE

CARLTON MELLICK III

The STEEL BREAKFAST ERA
a novel of the dark bizarre

Carlton Mellick III

Author OF RAZOR WIRE PUBIC HAIR

the Menstruating Mall

Carlton Mellick III

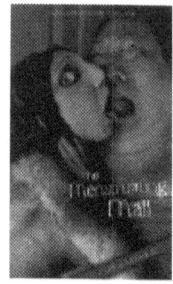  

Last Burn in Hell
by John Edward Lawson, 150 pgs

Kenrick Brimley is the state prison's official gigolo. From his romance with serial arsonist Leena Manasseh to his lurid angst-affair with a lesbian music diva, from his ascendance as unlikely pop icon to otherwordly encounters, the one constant truth is that he's got no clue what he's doing. As unrelenting as it is original, *Last Burn in Hell* is John Edward Lawson at his most scorching intensity, serving up sexy satire and postmodern pulp with his trademark day-glow prose.

Tempting Disaster edited by John Edward Lawson, 260 pgs

An anthology from the fringe that examines our culture's obsession with sexual taboos. Postmodernists and surrealists band together with renegade horror and sci-fi authors to re-envision what is "erotic" and what is "acceptable." By turns humorous and horrific, shocking and alluring, the authors dissect those impulses we deny in our daily lives. Includes stories by Carlton Mellick III, Michael Hemmingson, Lance Olsen & Jeffrey Thomas.

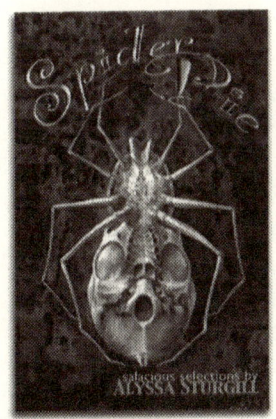

Spider Pie by Alyssa Sturgill, 104 pgs

Sturgill's debut book firmly establishes her as the *enfant terrible* of contemporary surrealism. Laden with gothic horror sensibilities, it's a one-way trip down a rabbit hole inhabited by sexual deviants and monsters, fairytale beginnings and hideous endings.